About the author

Apart from being a novelist, ˌ Green
(the Netherlands) has written collumns and ᵣₑₐₗₜₑ
pieces for national festivals and theatre groups. She
has also co-written radio plays (including an adap-
tion of Peter Buwalda's *Bonita Avenue*). Hendrix's
second book, *The Dyslexic Hearts Club*, was well-
received by literary critics and nominated for the
BNG Literary Award 2014. This road novel proved
to be a worthy successor to her debut *De verjaarda-
gen* (The Birthdays), which was shortlisted for the
Woman and Culture Prize, the Academica Debut
Prize and the Dioraphte Prize.

About the translator

David Doherty studied English and Literary Linguis-
tics in Glasgow before moving to the Netherlands,
where hc has been working as a translator for the
past 18 years. His translations include Jaap Robben's
debut novel *You Have Me to Love* (original title: *Birk*)
and *O, Louis. In Search of Louis van Gaal*, by Dutch
football writer Hugo Borst, which was shortlisted for
the 2015 British Sports Book Awards. He is currently
working on his third title for World Editions.

The Dyslexic Hearts Club

Hanneke Hendrix

The Dyslexic Hearts Club

Translated from the Dutch
by David Doherty

World Editions

Published in Great Britain in 2016 by World Editions Ltd., London

www.worldeditions.org

Copyright © Hanneke Hendrix, 2014
English translation copyright © David Doherty, 2016
Cover design Multitude
Image credit © Kate Abolins/Millennium Images/HH

First published as *De dyslectische-hartenclub* in the Netherlands in
2014 by De Geus BV, PO Box 1878, 4801 BW Breda

British Library Cataloguing-in-Publication Data
A catalogue record for this book is available on request from
the British Library

ISBN 978-94-6238-067-7

For all the friends I've lost along the way

There's an old joke. Two elderly women are at a Catskill mountain resort, and one of them says: 'Boy, the food at this place is really terrible.' The other one says: 'Yeah, I know. And such small portions.' Well, that's essentially how I feel about life. Full of loneliness and misery and suffering and unhappiness, and it's all over much too quickly. The other important joke for me is one that's usually attributed to Groucho Marx, but I think it appears originally in Freud's *Wit and Its Relation to the Unconscious*. And it goes like this—I'm paraphrasing: 'I would never want to belong to any club that would have someone like me for a member.'

ALVY SINGER, *Annie Hall* (1977)
Screenplay by Woody Allen and Marshall Brickman

You could point to moments earlier in my life when it all started to go wrong. But the more I think about it, the more I believe things really began to change the first time I saw Anna. That stuff about everyone sharing the blame is just soft talk from women's magazines, if you ask me. I don't buy it. Life is what happens to you. They'll tell you a person always has a choice, but that's not true. We're all just muddling along. There is no plan. The only clear sight is hindsight.

At first I lay for what seemed like ages in a room of my own. They kept it dark. Machines beeped. Cool hands touched me. Then I was moved. In silence they wheeled me down corridors, bumping me into a wall here, a door-post there. I counted the lights on the ceiling as I rattled along—twenty-one till I came to a halt and they turned my bed. A man in a police uniform sitting beside the door gave me a quick wave. I tried to guess his age but couldn't. Instead of waving back, I turned my head away and closed my eyes. The orderlies rolled me roughly into the room and when I opened my eyes again I was looking at a white curtain. As if I wasn't there, they hooked me up to a bunch of machines and left. The curtain stayed closed, the door clicked shut, and that's when I heard it: there were other people in here with me. Someone across from me and someone over to the right, each breathing heavily in their own way. Apart from that it was quiet. None of the hustle and bustle I had heard outside the room, no nurses chatting, no trolleys trundling past, no soles squeaking on linoleum. Nothing.

I must have dozed off, because suddenly I was jolted awake by a loud voice beside me.

'Anna van Veen?' said a nurse, sliding open my curtain an inch or two.

'Mrs Van Veen? Can you hear me?'

I nodded and lifted my hand to feel my head.

'Mrs Van Veen?' the nurse shouted a second time.

Her voice was piercing as well as loud. 'How are you feeling?'

'Fine,' I croaked.

I felt my side. Apart from a collapsed lung and assorted cuts and burns, things were looking up. The nurse ran her hands gingerly through my hair, examined the skin behind my ears, checked my bandages and the machine with the tube that burrowed into my body.

'There's no need to chain you up for the time being!'

The touch of her hands was as soft and gentle as her voice was loud.

'You'll be staying here for a while,' she hollered. 'With your new roommates. You're coming on a treat. Isn't that good news? Mrs Van Veen?'

I nodded. She smiled. I felt my head again and my fingertips tingled. The nurse smeared the bare patches on my scalp with dollops of Vaseline.

'They make this stuff from petroleum. Funny, isn't it? The thought of rubbing petroleum on burned skin always makes me chuckle. It's like magic. Don't you reckon, Mrs Van Veen?'

I shrugged. She spread some Vaseline on the stubble

where my eyebrows used to be and ran her thumb down my cheek. She smiled at me again.

'You're going to be just fine,' she said. 'You wait and see. I know these things.'

'Okay,' I said.

She jotted something down on the clipboard and hung it on the hook at the foot of my bed. I wanted to ask her how long I'd been here. I looked up at her.

'We'll leave the curtain closed for now,' she said. 'Give you time to get used to your new surroundings.'

I've never been a people person. I can't abide people who say they're a people person.

'Fine,' I said.

'Or would you like it open?'

I shook my head.

'Ring the bell if you need anything.'

She pointed to a red button beside my bed.

'If the button's working, that is,' she added. 'Those things don't always cooperate. The wiring around here has a habit of letting us down.'

I took another look at the button—a glowing red dot in a haze of white and beige. More than anything, I wanted to latch on to her white coat and beg her to take me back to my old room, where I'd been on my own. No TV, no magazines, only the beeping of the machines and the hum of the pumps and someone to give me the occasional once-over, as if checking a houseplant for greenfly. But I'm coming on a treat, or so she said. I should be happy. As she disappeared through the opening in the curtain, she turned around.

'So if no one comes it means the bell's not working and

you'll have to let out a good old-fashioned cry for help. Or you could always send Mrs Vandersteen to fetch the cavalry.'

I nodded.

'Sure you don't want a magazine to flick through?'

I shook my head.

'You can't get out of bed, you know, so once I'm gone you'll have nothing to do. Positive you don't want something to keep you occupied?'

I shook my head and thought about the tube sticking out of my side, and the daily ritual of the bedpan. What would that be like, now I had company? No sign of needing to go yet. That was something, at least. Perhaps some kind of distraction, just in case, wouldn't be such a bad idea. I spied a little notepad sticking out of her breast pocket and cleared my throat.

'Do you have a spare one of those?' I said softly.

She looked down at her breast pocket.

'Would you like to write something?' she asked.

I nodded, and she handed me the pad and a pencil.

Before they wheeled me in they had told me I was to be transferred to a secure hospital as soon as possible. They hadn't exactly showered me with tender loving care on the way here, rattling my bones every time they bumped the bed. Still I had survived, though perhaps that was the irony. Chances were I'd be sharing a cell before long. This was the lesser of two evils, most likely.

So by the sound of things there were two other people in the room. One kept hawking up phlegm. They didn't say a word to each other. For long stretches all I could hear was the turning of pages. The old magazines that do the rounds in hospitals, pages fingered by one set of hands, then another, then another, flicking through last week's news and gossip, killing time, the things you do in a place where all you can do is hope and wait. I heard gentle snoring, the sound of a TV through crackling old speakers. Now and then I heard the phlegmy woman shuffle over to the toilet for a pee. I lay there and listened in silence. Then I fell asleep.

I was woken up with a bang by the breakfast trolley, walloping through the door like a battering ram. During the night I'd had to ring for the bedpan. The nurse with the loud voice had shoved it resolutely under my backside—cold, hard, and fit for purpose. Her silence seemed to amplify the clatter. I'd been mortified by the thought of my roommates listening in, and though my bladder was fit to burst, it felt like a lifetime before the first drops began to flow. After that I'd slept soundly. No one came to visit. No visitors in the room on my own and none now that I was sharing with the others. I can't say I was surprised. I knew my place.

The breakfast trolley trundled past and the woman to my right was seized by a coughing fit. I glanced at the little clock on one of the machines beside my bed. Eight o'clock on the dot. I reached for my notepad, clamped the pencil between my teeth and began searching for words. *Dear Nelis*, I wrote. The person in charge of the trolley didn't say a thing. I couldn't help but notice. People don't like keeping quiet. There are rules and regulations for how much you should say. Safe margins. Saying nothing isn't good, but neither is saying too much. Be friendly to all and sundry, except for nutjobs. The nut-jobs of the world need to be put in their place so they know that they have to make more of an effort. I looked at the words on the page and decided this would only be a rough draft. I crossed out *Dear*. Then came the sound of plastic trays being slid onto bedside tables and liquid being poured into cups. Coffee.

My curtain was yanked aside. The runners in the rails gave a little shriek, as if they'd got a fright themselves. The nurse gave me a lingering look and I gazed over her shoulder in an attempt to avoid her eyes. Her ash-blonde hair was swept up into a big fat bun at the back of her head. You might have called her friendly, but for the telltale lines around her mouth that revealed she was no stranger to the fairground of mangled dreams. Six balls but never a coconut. Behind her I saw two doors and a washbasin. Everything here was beige.

'Good morning,' I sputtered. My voice was a creaky yodel.

The queen of the fairground maintained her silence and hurled the tray onto my bedside table with the steely conviction of a discus thrower. It was all I could do to halt its trajectory. The slices of bread skidded off the plate and my pencil rolled onto the floor. When I looked up she was standing to attention and holding two thermos flasks in the air. I didn't have a clue what she meant. She bobbed the flasks up and down impatiently.

'Oh,' I said. 'Of course.'

I pointed to the flask with the *T* on it. She poured. Perhaps she wasn't a nurse at all but a volunteer who helped out. A trauma victim who had lost the power of speech.

16

'Ah, just the ticket,' I said, to be friendly. 'Nothing beats a cuppa first thing in the morning.'

'Don't think you can sweet-talk me,' she said in a tone that thwacked me in the face like a rubber band. 'I know your type. And I'll do everything I can to make sure you're out of here as soon as possible. Fourteen forms I have to fill in for the privilege of bringing a sweaty slice of cheese to your bedside. So you can cut the sweetness-and-light routine. I know your type.'

With a bang—what was it with this place and banging everything around?—she slammed the flask back down on the trolley and snapped the curtain closed. The trolley trundled off and the door clunked shut. For a while all I could hear was chewing and slurping. A knife clinked on a plate, a cup was returned to its saucer, then everything went quiet. Somebody was thinking. I could feel it.

'An old writer once said… ' It was the phlegmy voice. 'I propose that from now on we defecate in public and eat our meals in private cubicles so no one has to see that filthy business. It's a view you share, Mrs Van Veen, unless I'm very much mistaken.'

I've spent my whole life feeling ill at ease. It's no big deal. That's just the way it is. I liked being on my own. Nelis used to say it was because I was an only child, but through the years I've met plenty of only children who have no trouble getting along with other people. I never saw the problem, but people always seemed to take offence at the fact that I didn't want to tag along, that I didn't look forward to office excursions with my husband's colleagues or weekends away with his family.

They would try to force me, make me join in the fun. I've never understood how that works, why people are so keen for you to join in when it's the last thing in the world you want.

'Everyone was asking after you,' Nelis would say when he got back.

When I stayed at home, people thought it reflected on them, that I meant something by it, that there was something wrong with them. You might think you're playing the lead, the star of your own show, but when it comes right down to it you're mostly just a bit player in other people's lives. That's how I see it, in any case.

'They can get along fine without me,' I'd reply. 'It's not like the party will grind to a halt because I'm not there.'

'That's not the point.'

'Exactly,' I said.

'Just you wait. There'll come a day when they won't ask you anymore. Then it'll be a different story.'

'Lost something?'

The curtain twitched open. To my right, a slight, spindly woman wearing reading glasses and a neat turtleneck of bandages peeped through, brandishing my pencil. I nodded. Pinkie raised, she held it between her long, thin fingers like an antique tin whistle, a relic from ancient Ireland.

'Are you a writer?' she asked.

I shook my head. The woman put the pencil to her lips and pretended to take a couple of drags. She leaned in slowly, took the pencil from her mouth and said, 'I'd kill for a cigarette.'

I swallowed.

'I know you can speak,' she said, shuffling closer. 'So don't go playing the deaf mute. We've got one of those already.'

She nodded over her shoulder at the room's third occupant, still hidden behind the curtain. 'Yes, you heard me!' she yelled. 'I'm talking about you!'

The spindly woman laid the pencil on my lap. I reckoned she must be about fifty. I still don't know how old she is. It's hard to imagine Vandersteen being born. More likely she appeared out of nowhere one day. Bam! There she stood in a puff of smoke, dusted herself down, and she was up and running. She shook me firmly by the hand.

'Vandersteen,' she said.

'Mrs Van Veen,' I said.

'Yes, that much I'd heard,' she said. 'Our pal over there doesn't have a name.'

'Oh,' I said, wondering whether she was a nutjob or whether to be friendly.

'It says "Ms X" on her chart. I've already had a good read. The Grouch and Megaphone Mary don't know who she is, either. The nurses, I mean.'

'Is she conscious?' I asked.

'Of course she's conscious,' said Vandersteen, and shouted over her shoulder again. 'She can hear me, all right!'

'Apart from that we get along fine,' she continued, returning to normal volume. 'I think it's safe to say she's just a girl. Can't be much more than twenty. It's not easy to tell. The burns are pretty bad.'

'Gosh,' I said.

'Sounds like you haven't won any prizes for your extensive vocabulary either.'

I cleared my throat and looked at her. I had picked up the pencil from my lap and started fidgeting with it. Vandersteen crossed her arms and gazed at me intently. There was nothing alarming in her stare. It was friendly, if anything.

'Have you been here long?' I said at last.

'A week or so. Two, three, four, five. After a while you lose count. In hospital, that is. Only moved to this room yesterday.'

Across the room I could hear Ms X breathing, slowly in through her nose and then out again in short sharp bursts.

'What about her?' I pointed across the room, hesitantly, though I knew Ms X couldn't see me.

'They wheeled her in here yesterday, too. Oh good, I thought, company at last. How wrong can you be? And then you arrived.'

'I was in a room on my own at first,' I said.

'Did you prefer it that way?'

I shrugged.

'After a while you cost too much.'

'True,' said Vandersteen. 'And what do you reckon to that policeman parked outside our door?'

'Huh?' I said. There had been a policeman parked outside my other room, too, but Vandersteen didn't need to know that.

'A copper,' said Vandersteen. 'Moustache and everything. Been sat there from the moment they wheeled Tubby in.'

'Tubby?' I said.

Vandersteen pointed at the curtain without unfolding her arms.

'Ms X.'

'Oh,' I said.

'And you're a burns patient, too,' said Vandersteen. 'That makes three of us. Tubby's worst off. Her face is burned. But she's already on the mend. You're not in such a bad way. I could tell straight off. I worked in this hospital for years. How old are you? Let me guess. I have a knack. Thirty-four? Am I right? Are you thirty-four?'

'Doesn't she mind?' I asked. 'You calling her "Tubby" all the time?'

'Let's face it, either you're tubby or you're not,' said Vandersteen. 'I could just as easily *not* say it, but what would that change? I mean, if I called *you* tubby that would be nasty because you're not exactly tubby but you're not exactly slim either. How much do you weigh?'

I mumbled something.

'155 pounds? 160?'

She raised her reading glasses and shot me an inquiring look.

'150 pounds,' I said quickly.

'See what I mean... 155,' said Vandersteen.

I wanted to tell her she was talking rubbish, tell her to button it and go back to bed.

'If you say so,' I replied.

'So now we have two young ladies, one old bag, and a copper with a 'tache posted at the door. If you ask me, it was Miss Scarlet in the library with a candlestick.'

Vandersteen started banging on about the policeman not letting her out of the room for a smoke and refusing to even answer when she asked him why.

'But surely they can't just hold you here against your will, Mrs Vandersteen?' I said.

I started fidgeting with the sheet. The closed curtain was making me claustrophobic, what with Vandersteen in here with me, and knowing I couldn't make a move with that tube in my side.

'You're a sweetheart,' said Vandersteen. 'I can tell just by looking at you. And for God's sake, drop the "Mrs." With all these bandages I already feel like I've been scraped out of a sarcophagus.'

Vandersteen slipped back through the curtains and I caught a glimpse of a window. Clear blue sky. Somewhere on the other side of the building the sun must be shining. I thought of my last afternoon on the houseboat. It had been a warm afternoon, late summer. I had spent the whole day sitting out on the deck reading a book. I can't remember the title. Funny that: you spend hours reading a book, a whole world is conjured up inside your head, and afterwards you can't remember a thing about it. Not a thing. So you can't even ask someone, 'What was the name of that book again? You know, the one with the farmer and his wife and that remote country estate, and that murder and all those pigs.' I can't remember a thing about it. I can see myself sitting there, trouser legs rolled up, dipping a toe in the water. I'm holding a book and I can almost make out the letters, but that's as far as I get before it all slides out of focus. The cover remains a black rectangle, black as an old Bible.

'Well,' said Vandersteen, after I'd heard her climb back into bed. 'It's a bundle of laughs sharing a room with you two chatterboxes. We should start a pub and call it The Twitchy Hip. That way everyone will know… '

She paused.

'Everyone'll know… '

Another pause.

'Twitchy? Hip? Don't all shout at once… '

I wondered whether I should say something.

'No takers? We'll call it The Twitchy Hip, so everyone'll know… there's one joint that's *really* jumping. Geddit? Geddit?'

The silence was deafening.

A few minutes later Vandersteen was snoring softly.

I asked the loud nurse to open the curtain for me. She took hold of the edge and gave me a wink.

'Sure you're up to it?' she shouted. 'Not worried that the ladies will disappoint?'

She laughed a loud tinkling laugh.

'I can hear you, you know,' Vandersteen muttered.

The runners slid slowly over the rail to reveal a stretch of wall, an open green-and-orange curtain, and then a square of sky, blue, with a cloud or two. The sun was shining. A bird flew past. Vandersteen was sitting upright in bed, with the windows directly behind her. She looked twig-like under her sheet, and the sunshine formed a halo around her head. In one hand she was holding a gossip magazine—the cover showed a girl being kissed by a prince. Bathed in light, Vandersteen looked like a miniature god. I had to squint to make her out. She made as if to wave, but she'd barely lifted her hand before she erupted into a coughing fit.

'That's roommate number one!' shouted the nurse.

I waved at Vandersteen, still coughing as she lunged for the tissues on her bedside table. The curtain continued its journey along the rail, and Tubby appeared. A colossus wrapped in shiny red skin, half-hidden under an enormous pile of bedclothes. It was as if someone had screwed off her nose and her ears and painted over her face with red enamel. Tubby was a fortress, a citadel, a breakwater, an island rising out of the sea, or all of those things put together. Someone had tried to burn the fortress to the ground, but by the look of things they hadn't succeeded.

'Hi,' I said.

I waved. She waved back. I tried not to let the shock show on my face.

'That's your lot,' said the nurse. 'Happy?'

I nodded.

'Then I'm happy, too,' she replied, and left the room. All at once I noticed how little space we were sharing. I reckoned the breakfast trolley could only just fit between the foot of my bed and Tubby's across from me.

'Is this a double room?' I asked.

'Well spotted,' said Vandersteen. 'They're short on rooms with private facilities. And without them, our guardian angel out there would have to escort us to the toilet, as well. When I used to work here, we sometimes had to improvise and shift everything around, too. Not ideal, but what can you do? Could be worse. I'm doing just fine over here at the window.'

Tubby closed her eyes and folded her hands. I couldn't tell if she was sleeping or praying.

'Dearie me,' said the grouchy nurse as she changed the sheets on Tubby's bed. The door was open. I could just see the copper's legs out in the corridor.

'Do you realize it takes a nurse an extra eight minutes to tend to a patient who's seriously overweight? Do you? No, you can't talk, granted. But it's true. You're costing us an arm and a leg. Money that could have been better spent if you'd only learned to control your urges. Swallowed your tongue as well, have you?'

Tubby stood barefoot on the lino, bashful in her white nightgown. She looked helplessly toward the windows, where Vandersteen lay snoring.

'I have to clean and talc all those folds of skin. And I'm not even talking about the burns. Nothing you can do about those, after all.'

I heard chuckling coming from the corridor, and saw the copper's legs move. The grouchy nurse looked up, irritated.

'But who has to lift all those flaps, hold them up and go at the creases with a damp cloth?'

Tubby looked at me. I gave what I hoped was a sympathetic shrug with my right shoulder.

'Do you know,' said the grouchy nurse as she whipped the bottom sheet from the bed, 'why so few nurses are overweight?'

Because they're not sitting at a desk all day, I thought. Tubby turned her gaze away from me. 'Because day in, day out, we see how much trouble it is to scrub down all that fat.'

Furiously, she tugged the clean sheets over the bed.

'Less grub, more exercise,' she said. 'It's as simple as that.'

'So beer's out, too, is it?' said Vandersteen, out of nowhere.

The nurse squeezed out a short laugh.

'Ha! That's worst of all,' she said. 'Beer.'

She spat out the word as if Vandersteen had said 'dead foetus.'

'Beer! You'd be better off chomping your way through a box of chocolate éclairs.'

'And you reckon that's right, do you?' said Vandersteen.

'Of course it's right. Alcohol's of no earthly use to anyone. Good for cleaning though, I'll give it that.'

'No, I mean, do you reckon it's right to talk to that girl the way you're talking to her.'

The nurse pointed testily at the bed. Tubby climbed in, sat up, and the nurse set about tucking in the bedclothes.

'I'm just telling it like it is. I'm not one to beat around the bush or take pity. Pity's the worst. Drown everyone in pity and nothing will ever get done. It's no use to any patient, no matter what state they're in. Besides, I've every right to speak my mind, especially when I'm speaking the truth.'

'No, that's not what you're doing at all,' said Vandersteen. 'You're shooting your mouth off so you can feel better about yourself. There's the truth for you, scraggy bag of bones that you are.'

Her words hung in the air. The grouchy nurse narrowed her eyes. 'Takes one to know one.'

'Van Veen,' said Vandersteen. 'Anything to say for yourself?'

The nurse was tucking Tubby in way too tight.

'Uh… yes,' I said. 'What you just said… I agree.'

'I'm going to rise above this,' said the nurse. 'And not say another word.'

She thrust Tubby forward, shook her pillow, and pushed her back against it. Then she marched out of the room. Tubby hung her head. I picked up my notepad. Vandersteen put down her magazine.

'Listen up, you two,' she said. 'That's not how things are going to work around here.'

I counted the lines on the page in front of me. As a kid, back on the island, I used to count the boards that lined the wall of our holiday cottage whenever there was an awkward moment. 'This isn't the house of straw, it's the house of sticks,' my father used to say. At that point my mother usually reminded him it wasn't a house of bricks either. There were twenty-three boards on the wall where the fireplace was, the wall opposite the settee: eleven up to the window, four short ones under the window, and then another eight. I counted them over and over again. The answer was always the same. When it was dark, we closed the shutters. As a kid that was my idea of cosy.

'Let's get one thing straight: I'm not going to be the one to stand up for everybody. Tubs, you need to find a way to shut a witch like that up. You can't just stand there and nod while she hurls insults at you.'

Tubby sighed.

'Every word she said was about her, not about you. You understand that, don't you, love?'

'Yes,' I said. 'That's true.'

'Well if it isn't Van Veen, back from the dead,' Vandersteen snapped. 'Do you hear what I'm saying, Tubs?'

Tubby nodded.

'We have to look out for one another,' said Vander-steen.

'You're right,' I said. 'Sorry.'

I felt ashamed. Vandersteen went back to her gossip mag. I picked up my pencil and looked at the two words I'd committed to paper. I'd crossed out *Dear* and then written *Dear* again above it. After that I'd crossed out *Nelis*. Maybe I'd be better off watching TV. *Dear, I don't know if you know how I'm doing but things are looking up*, I wrote. I looked at the words, tore off the page, crumpled it into a ball, and fired it at the wastepaper basket. Hole in one. I looked up. No one had seen. Tubby had closed her eyes again.

'Hole in one?' asked Vandersteen, without taking her eyes off her magazine.

'Yup,' I said proudly.

I turned my attention to the empty lines on the page, fourteen in all. Later on, I'd count the pages. There were two hundred, including the one in the wastepaper basket. The copper out in the corridor went into convulsions, coughing long and deep.

In the evening we watched TV. The only television in the room hung between the two big windows, directly above Vandersteen's head. If she knelt on her bed she could turn it on. Vandersteen was an aficionado. She rolled her bedclothes to the foot of her bed, propped her pillow up against them, and plopped herself down.

'Aah,' she said. 'Welcome to the TV suite.'

The theme tune to the daily showbiz news round-up bounced across the room. It was Vandersteen's favourite. She sipped at her tumbler of water as if it was a glass of Chartreuse.

'Look,' she said. 'There she is. Mariska Kampschreur. You must've heard of her?'

'Yes,' I said.

We didn't have a TV on the houseboat, but everyone had heard of Mariska Kampschreur. A few years back she had abandoned serious journalism to become the face of early-evening light entertainment. Our newspaper had accused her of selling out for the big bucks. I'd told Nelis I understood where she was coming from, that there comes a time when it's all about paying that big fat mortgage, but I was really only saying it to wind him up. She should've got herself a smaller house, that's what I really thought about Mariska Kampschreur and her career move. Nelis said you could never take anyone seriously once they had sold their soul to the devil. I said it made sense to me. Of course, I didn't know then what I know now.

I watched along with Vandersteen. Kampschreur had a stiff blonde hairdo, like one of those Playmobil figures. The longer I watched, the more it struck me that she was really enjoying herself. A new item was just getting started. A tall man had pulled up a chair to talk about a pop starlet and her nightmare nose job. Vandersteen clamped her tumbler between her spindly legs and clapped her hands with glee.

'Pride and vanity,' she nattered. 'Pride and vanity. But they can work miracles nowadays, you know. Blood miracles. She'll be back next week with a brand-new nose, just wait and see. Another chance to plug her new album.'

Tubby was watching, too, the skin on her face shining. The fire had consumed part of her nose and ears. She was wearing a white cap, so I couldn't tell if she still had hair. The shiny red skin continued down her neck and disappeared under her nightgown. She tossed and turned wildly in her dreams, but during our first days together in that room she didn't utter a sound. Her hands lay in her lap. They seemed relatively unscathed and she always had them folded, as if she was sitting in a church pew. In spite of her silence, I could see she was a smart girl, the same way you can tell the bright kids from the thick kids before they can even talk. It's the look in their eyes. Nelis once said that's where it all went wrong with us humans: as soon as we started talking, we stopped being part of our surroundings. I loved him so much when he came out with things like that. Tubby's mouth merged into tough red skin that pulled her lips so tight it seemed to be an effort for her to close them. When I looked closer, I noticed her lips were moving slightly. She seemed to be murmuring to herself.

'The paparazzi hounded Mariska for ages, snapping away like mad,' said Vandersteen.

Tubby's lips suddenly stopped moving, and I quickly turned to look at the TV again. A man with a magic marker was drawing a line on a woman's face.

'They could cut and paste all they wanted, but they never got a juicy story out of her. Not a sausage. She has wo dogs and a successful media company. That's yer lot. No husband, no wife, nada. I reckon she's asexual, like that Cliff Richards fella. Convenient, if you ask me. Spares you all kinds of trouble.'

The final credits raced across the screen. Vandersteen turned around and asked if we wanted to watch anything else. I shook my head. She clicked off the TV and, with much flapping of blankets and sheets, made her way from the TV suite back to the bedroom.

'What a woman,' she sighed as she settled back against her pillows. 'I'd marry her in a heartbeat. This minute. Today.'

'Who?' I said. 'Mariska what's-her-face?'

Vandersteen nodded.

'Give me a strong woman any day. I've never been able to live with a man. Believe me, I've tried. I was born in the Stone Age, after all. But I'm too much of a handful for them.'

She glanced out the window.

'That said, I'd probably have to morph into a pooch to stand a chance with Mariska.'

'It takes all sorts,' I said.

'Have you got a husband?' asked Vandersteen.

I didn't reply.

'No need to act all la-di-da with that notepad of yours. Don't think I haven't noticed that you've barely written two words.'

'No, I don't have a husband,' I said. 'You?'

'Wife,' said Vandersteen.

'Can't say I've seen her around,' I said.

'I *had* a wife,' said Vandersteen.

'Oh,' I said.

31

Silence. Tubby breathed steadily through her nose, in out, in out, and Vandersteen flicked through her magazines. I thought about what I should do. I had plenty of time for pondering, but there was no sign of a conclusion. I thought a lot about home, about our houseboat in the docks at the edge of town. About Nelis. His hands, his eyes, the way he spoke, the way he drank his coffee. Every time he made a fresh pot he used to note the time and leave the note by the coffee machine. Fresh coffee was the only law in our home. 'Coffee's a religion,' he once said. With him around, everything felt warm and cosy. I know I'll never get him back, of course I do, but looking back now I'd give anything to undo what happened. Even though I'd have no idea where to begin. Perhaps as far back as the island. But here I was, lying in a hospital room under police guard and thinking about what I should do. One idea throbbed in my head all day, like a migraine: I've got to get out of here.

'Beans, spuds, and fish, our favourite Friday dish,' sang Vandersteen. It was lunch, our one hot meal of the day. 'No visitors for you two, either, then?'

She tilted her head and peered at me through her reading glasses. I poked my fork at the battered fish that had fallen to pieces on my plate.

'It's Thursday,' I said.

'Yeah, yeah, they're not that strict in these parts,' said Vandersteen. 'No cards? No one had a card yet? Tubs? You neither? A young thing like you.'

Vandersteen shook her head.

'It's a regular vale of tears around here.'

I speared a spud and followed it up with a flake or two of fish and a bean. I took a look at my forkful and shoved it into my mouth. Nelis said I had a dyslexic heart, which always made me think of the girl who sat next to me in primary school. She was dyslexic, and annoying with it. I suppose the fact that I can't remember her name even though I sat beside her all those years proves Nelis's point.

'I know exactly what makes you tick,' he told me once. 'But you can't read me.'

He had a point there, too.

I was cycling home, shortly after dark, pedalling over the dyke all the way to the docks. Nothing beats a summer bike ride in the cool of the evening. I'd been to a hunting trade fair in Belgium and I'd been planning to spend the night in a hotel, but the fair hadn't been up to much, so I'd taken a late train home instead. Our houseboat was moored at the industrial docks, the cheapest spot in town. There was an abattoir right next door, pigs mostly. An old-fashioned slaughterhouse built beyond the city limits and then gradually swallowed up by urban expansion, till now it lay just outside the centre. If you could sketch a smell, I'd be able to draw the smell of the slaughterhouse for you now with my eyes closed: feed silos mixed with the odour of an old fridge left unplugged with the door closed for a very long time. Our neighbour called the council every time he caught a whiff of offal, which was between two and six times a day, depending on the wind. I swooped from the dyke down into the docks with my head in the breeze. Almost home, I thought. A lorry was chuntering away outside the abattoir's big warehouse door, a cheery family of pigs emblazoned on the side. Porkers in the pink of health.

It was a beautiful evening. With the abattoir behind me, there was only our neighbour's barge to cycle past. He always left a string of coloured fairy lights on in the summer, even when he was on holiday. The warm glow of homecoming began when I laid eyes on them. I braked at the gangplank to our boat, that old floating wooden bungalow of ours, and chained my bike to the lamppost. It was quiet. No coots, no pigs, no yelling from the drunks who liked to loll about on the bench at the end of the dyke. Not a sound. On the boat, the lights were out.

That was odd.

The car was parked outside, as usual. Nelis's bike was there, too, chained to the mailbox. Next door's fairy lights swayed in the breeze. I was filled with longing for my own bed. Curling up in your own bed—come to think of it, that even trumps a summer-evening bike ride.

I walked up the gangplank. I couldn't remember Nelis saying he had anything on that evening, but wherever he'd gone, he must have decided to go on foot. I reached for my keys, opened the front door, dropped my bag in the hall, and went into the living room. Then I heard something. It came from the other side of the boat. He's ill, I thought. There's something wrong. I walked over to the bedroom. The door was ajar and the neighbour's lights cast dim colours on the bed. The curtains were open—I liked them open, Nelis didn't. Just as I was about to enter the room, I realized there was someone else in

34

bed with him. In the glow of the fairy lights I saw Nelis's pale backside heaving up and down. I jumped. Without making a sound, I stepped back into the hall.

A strange kind of thrill flared up inside me.

The thought came a fraction of a second later: I knew it. I knew it all along. He doesn't love me. And now he's going to pay for that feeling I've had my whole life, the feeling that there's something wrong. For a moment I was grateful. Relieved. I saw a way out, a fleeting glimpse of another life: the apartment I'd rent, my birds in every room, the neighbourhood I'd live in, never having to make allowances for someone else. Alone, alone at last.

I stood there in the hall, thinking, and heard his deep voice murmuring in the background like a mantra. I only heard her for a second—a solitary whimper, that was all. Then the pain came flooding in. The rejection. I turned and walked away, hitched my bag over my shoulder, opened the front door, trod quietly over the gangplank to my bike, and cycled to the far side of the abattoir. I called him, left a message, and within ten minutes the windows on the boat lit up. A shadow ran down the gangplank and disappeared in the direction of the dyke.

I cycled home in slow motion. With much clunking and rattling, I chained my bike to the mailbox.

'Not much fun to be had?' Nelis called from the doorway.

'Meh,' I said. 'I just felt like coming home.'

'I'm glad,' he said.

'Me too,' I said.

You prick, I thought, but I said nothing. I sat down on

the couch and asked if there was any coffee going. 'No,' he said. 'I've already rinsed out the pot.'

Then he went to bed. I don't know what happens to a person when they imagine no one can see them, like me at that moment, when no one knew that I knew what I knew. I was sure I'd have no trouble acting as if nothing had happened. I didn't have a plan. There are times when I wish I was smarter. Maybe in my next life.

Funny thing is, that next life is now.

I had it all under control. I'll bide my time, I thought. I didn't do anything out of the ordinary. It's an interesting feeling when you start acting your own life. He gave a sterling performance, too, mind you. Never let anything slip. But I was one step ahead. I knew about him, and I knew he didn't know that I knew. It came naturally, the acting. Like slipping into an old pair of shoes I hadn't worn for a while. Your feet recognize the lumps and hollows in the insoles. I didn't know exactly how, but I was going to throw it in his face, and I was relishing the prospect. A while back we had planned a party for his birthday. I'm not one for throwing parties, but he was turning forty, so I'd surprised him and said it was fine by me if he invited everyone around to celebrate.

I had meant it.

He was so happy.

'So you had a wife?' I asked Vandersteen.

'You betcha,' said Vandersteen. 'I was married to Angelique. But we split up. Only a month ago. Officially.'

Vandersteen was perched on her bed. Her twiggy legs dangled over the edge, swinging to and fro under pale, bony knees. Tubby stared into space.

'It wasn't what you'd call a success,' said Vandersteen. 'Well, put it this way, I thought it was a success, but after a while she'd had enough of me.'

'Really?' I asked. 'Were you a handful?'

'I would appear to be a rather restless individual.'

Outside, the sun broke through a heavy rain cloud. A pigeon landed on the windowsill. Vandersteen slid off the bed and tapped the window.

'Hello, my little dove,' she said.

The pigeon flew off.

'Flying rats,' she muttered.

'Pigeons are actually very smart,' I informed her.

I must have been around ten. I was with my father, and we were watching the chickens that scratched around the edge of the woods near our holiday cottage. My father explained that if you kept chickens in a run, you had to clip their wings or they'd start to fly. The wings of our woodland chickens weren't yet long enough to allow them to fly. Or perhaps they'd just forgotten how.

'It doesn't hurt when you clip them,' my father said. 'It's like us getting our hair cut.'

'Does that mean chickens would fly around, other-wise?' I asked.

My father thought for a while, then patted me gently on the head. A cock crowed somewhere in among the trees.

'Not really,' he said. 'If they flap like mad, they can just about clear a fence, and even then they look awkward. They're not like geese. They don't want to head south in winter.'

I pictured a flock of chickens high in sky.

Taxidermy is my first love. Birds, especially. On our houseboat I set aside a room as a workshop for my animals. Occasionally I had to rent extra workspace, like the time when that moose head wouldn't fit through the front door. I'm not fussy—for money I'll stuff anything, but left to my own devices it would always be birds. Chickens are my favourite. There's something simple and honest about them. My husband gave me that warm, cosy feeling, and for whatever reason, so did my birds. For me there was nothing finer than coming home, walking into my room, and flopping down in an armchair with the ladies and gents of the avian world looking down from the walls around me. At the far end of the room stood my workbench and a desk for my computer. Ideally I'd have had separate rooms: a showroom, a workshop, and an office, but Nelis had banned my feathered family from the rest of the boat. I can understand that. You can't share everything. Perhaps that's what did for us in the end.

'I'm not crazy,' said Vandersteen. 'I make a good partner. When I stand by someone, I stand by them forever. Whether they still want me by their side or not. One day I found two empty trunks in the hall, and a note that said she was catching a train to her mother's and taking the kids with her. She gave me a week to pack my things. She hadn't been gone long—I could tell because she'd left that day's post on the sideboard. I ran outside to see if I could catch sight of her. Jesus, it must have been minus ten out there. Did I leave? Are you kidding? I wasn't about to wander off into the wilderness just like that. She'll miss me, I thought, and by the time she comes back it'll all be okay.'

'You've got kids?'

'We've got kids.'

'How many?'

'Two.'

'Oh, that's nice,' I said.

'Yes,' said Vandersteen.

'What are their names?'

Vandersteen looked out the window and bit her fingernail.

'God, I could do with a ciggie,' she said.

She breathed against the windowpane and drew a cock and balls in the little patch of condensation.

'When Angelique came back she said I made the kids nervous,' said Vandersteen. 'Who knows, maybe it was true. And so I left, after all. But I still believe we could have sorted things out between us, given half a chance.'

She went over and sat back down on her bed.

'I think.'

'Hmmmm,' I said.

'Pffff,' she sighed. 'Women. You're better off keeping chickens. Or pigeons, for that matter.'

I thought of Nelis. I imagined leaving two trunks at the front door for him, and how, once he'd gone, I could have spread my birds all around the boat and sat there gazing contentedly over the water at the coots paddling by in the harbour, parping away like party tooters.

'Are you still allowed to see the kids?' I asked.

'I don't know,' said Vandersteen.

She puffed out her cheeks and let the air slowly escape.

'Ten years we'd been together. I wanted to talk but she wouldn't give an inch. Maybe I'd become a bit of an old biddy. I don't know. I spent a lot of time at home. But to slam the door shut like that… '

'Kids have short memories.'

'I haven't seen them for months. Not since winter.'

'Have you been in here all that time?' I asked.

'Eh… no, a few things have happened in the meantime. But if she called me up and said, "Come on home, love," I'd be there like a shot.'

'Unless Mariska Kampschreur calls you up first,' I said.

Vandersteen laughed.

'Yep, that would be a game-changer, all right.'

'I can picture it now, picking up the phone and hearing that deep womanly voice and those mangy little mutts of hers yapping away in the background. "Could I speak to Vandersteen please?"'

'And then I come to the phone,' said Vandersteen.

'Yes,' I said. 'You come a-running and grab the receiver off me and say: "It's me, it's me!" And then that sultry voice says… 'I do my best Dietrich. '"Vandersteen, honey lamb, will you marry me?"'

'Aahh, wouldn't that be grand… '

'Yes,' I said. 'That's one wedding I wouldn't want to miss.'

'Well then, we'll need to make sure it happens.'

For a moment we sat there, chuckling. For a moment there was only that. Vandersteen reached for the fresh pile of outdated magazines brought in by the loud nurse that morning.

'I don't have anyone, either,' I said. 'Not anymore.'

Vandersteen's hand hovered in mid-air above her bedside table.

'So we're there now, are we?' she said.

'Where?' I asked.

'At the point where we finally get to talk about you?'

I shrugged.

'Maybe,' I said.

'I've been dying of curiosity over here,' said Vandersteen.

'What do you want to know?'

'Are your parents still alive?'

'No,' I said. 'They're dead.'

'Oh,' said Vandersteen. 'Sorry.'

'That's okay,' I said. 'It's not like I ever saw them much.'

'Brothers? Sisters?'

'No,' I said.

'Friends?'

'I'm not really one for friends,' I said.

'All alone,' said Vandersteen.

'Pretty much,' I said.

'What a shame. A fine bunch of women like us. Yes, you too, Tubs. I mean, I'm an old bag, but the two of you…'

'I reckon we're both glad to have you around,' I said.

'Yeah, okay, as old bags go, I'm a corker. Don't look a day over two hundred. But still. If I'd died at home it would've been ten years before they found me, a length of parchment in an armchair next to the radiator. Under the standard lamp, still clutching a magazine. Maybe not such a bad way to go.'

'I'd sign up for that,' I said.

Vandersteen nodded.

'What about your visitors, Tubs?' asked Vandersteen.

Tubby gave a cautious shrug.

'Not expecting anyone? Our personal bodyguard at the door isn't sitting there for the good of his health.'

Vandersteen's voice sounded much gentler than normal.

'It's almost enough to make you think that someone around here is expecting someone to turn up, eh?'

Tubby shook her head sadly. A drop of water tapped onto her sheet, a big fat tear. Vandersteen slid off her bed, jumped up next to Tubby, and put her arm around her—a scrawny little arm around Tubby's broad shoulders. Vandersteen hummed a little tune. Tubby sighed again, a very deep sigh this time, and carefully rested her cheek on Vandersteen's head. They sat there for a long while. There are times when you can sense that other people are feeling the same thing you are. We shared the silence. I reached for my notepad, and this time I didn't count the lines on the page or the tiles above the washbasin. In this moment everything seemed to fall into place, everything we had been through, how alone we all were. Everything I had done, everything that had happened to the other two, even though at that point I didn't know the details. And to be honest, now that I think about it, the details hardly matter anymore.

It happened that night. After the three of us had switched off our lamps and all we could see were clouds drifting across the moon, Tubby decided to talk.

'Okay,' she said softly.

Vandersteen and I both sat up at once. I could make out Tubby's silhouette against the shadows that played across the curtain.

'Okay,' she said again, even more softly this time.

'Lo,' said Vandersteen. 'It speaks.'

I hissed at Vandersteen to be quiet.

'My name's Anna, too,' she said.

Her voice was thin.

'And it has a beautiful name into the bargain,' said Vandersteen.

'Believe it or not, I'm a right old chatterbox,' Anna whispered sadly.

'That's fine, love,' said Vandersteen. 'Welcome here among us. We've missed you.'

I nodded, though I knew no one else could see.

The next day they removed my drain, and for the first time I was able to go to the toilet by myself. I wanted to look in the mirror, but all the mirrors had been taken down. For the first time in ages I could sit and do my business without someone hearing me, or having to slide a bedpan under me. I sat on the toilet with my chin in my hands, listening to Vandersteen singing softly to herself as she sat in bed. Now it was only a matter of time before I would be transferred. Criminal proceedings were already underway, and soon I'd be well enough for a prison cell. I no longer wanted to be cooped up all by myself.

There was something about being with the other two that made me want to stay.

I came out of the toilet to find Vandersteen with one ear pressed to the front door.

'What are you doing?' I said.

'I think they're on a break,' Vandersteen whispered.

'The copper, too?' I asked.

'Nah, he's still there, but I'll take my chances.'

She scampered over to the window and whipped out a cigarette.

'Ta-daaaa,' she said.

'How did you get your hands on that?' I said.

'I have my methods. They don't call me the Artful Dodger for nothing.'

'Watch yourself,' I said. 'That copper'll be onto you before you know it.'

'He's not sat out there for my benefit,' said Vandersteen. 'You strike me as the criminal type, though... '

I let out a short and sharp 'Ha.'

'Nervous little laugh,' said Vandersteen. 'Suspiciously so.'

'It takes one... ' I said. 'Well? Well?'

'What are you on about?' said Vandersteen.

'It takes one... ' I said again.

'Oh, give it a rest,' said Vandersteen. 'I don't mind admitting I've been in the clink.'

I threw my head back and laughed so loud, I could feel it resonate in my stomach.

'What were you in for?' I asked.

'My dear,' said Vandersteen. 'You name it, I've been

done for it. Murder, rape, and manslaughter excepted.'

She thought for a moment.

'Yup, apart from those three I've got the full set. And I'm not ashamed of any of it. Back in the old days, breaking the law was more like high jinks. Yer ruthless, hard-nosed life of crime never appealed to me much. I'm a socialist. Maybe even a pacifist, too, if you only have to tick eight out of ten boxes to qualify.'

'Pure as the driven snow,' I said.

'Scouts' honour,' said Vandersteen.

'Like that counts for anything with your rap sheet,' I said.

'As the years went by, I got a little too old be on the run from the police.'

'Is it lunchtime yet?' I asked.

'Time to change the subject, you mean?' said Vandersteen.

'Yes,' I said.

'Fair enough,' said Vandersteen. 'I've worked in nearly every hospital you can name. Will that do you as a subject? Cleaning. Nursing. Never stay long. I get bored easily. Attention span of a flea. That's 'cause I grew up in a toyshop.'

I sat bolt upright.

'Really?' I said.

'We lived right upstairs,' said Vandersteen.

'Wow,' I said.

'Anything I wanted to play with was mine for the taking. Guaranteed to make a complete brat of you,' said Vandersteen.

She yanked open the curtain and knocked on the windowpane.

'We're a long way up. You can see the entire car park from here.'

Vandersteen reckoned we were in a quiet ward up on the top floor. According to her theory, this was a room for quarantine patients, hence the private bathroom and the door you could seal off if you had to. She pointed at the cars below.

'Look long enough and things start to fall into place. Some cars come every day. The odd-coloured ones and the snazzy old-timers are easiest to keep track of. There's a little old man who comes every day and stays exactly twenty-five minutes. He walks very slowly and drives one of those red biscuit tins with a crumple zone that ends somewhere in the back seat. Never take a lift in a car like that: crash into a toddler at walking pace and you're a goner. Wouldn't surprise me if it's an automatic to boot. Bloody nightmare. How anyone can drive a pile of junk like that is beyond me.'

'I don't have a licence,' Anna whispered.

'You barely need one to drive one of those things. Dodgems they are. If we ever get out of here, I'll teach you to drive a proper car. Or a truck, for that matter. I've got my heavy goods licence. Handy if you ever need to shift a consignment of dream kitchens.'

'Of what?' I said.

Tubby chuckled.

Vandersteen straightened her glasses.

'Steady on, Tubs,' she said.

I burst out laughing, too. All day long I found myself laughing at any old thing. I was inquisitive. I was cheer-ful. What the hell was wrong with me? Were they slipping happy pills into my food? Perhaps it was just a side effect of feeling better every day, though that same thought was a worry nagging away at the back of my mind.

'What does he do? The little old man?' asked Anna.

'If you ask me, his wife's in hospital. She's either senile or in a coma, but he makes himself come and visit every day because that's the kind of man he is.'

Vandersteen drew quotation marks in the air when she said 'kind of man.'

'A man of principle. Not that anyone cares about his principles. No one can stand him. He always comes alone and leaves alone, so he doesn't have any children who are close, if he has any at all. At the pace he walks, and knowing how far it is to the geriatric ward or intensive care, I'd say that leaves between five and eight minutes for his wife. As soon as he's pulled up a chair at her bedside he's already thinking about leaving. He probably mutters a few "dearie mes" and "my, mys", drinks a cup of tea, and then he's off again. That's what I reckon. She's lost the power of speech, quite a contrast 'cause he's the kind of man with a wife who never used to shut up, who'd keep on babbling even if you were standing there with one foot out the door. I can't abide that kind of woma...'

Vandersteen abruptly stopped babbling.

'Jesus,' she said. 'I talk a load of bollocks sometimes. Sorry.'

I slid out of bed and joined her at the window.

'What a prick,' she said, with her arms crossed.

The door to the room swung wide and the grouchy nurse made her entrance.

'I see. No sooner are we out of bed than we're over

standing at the window,' she said as she wheeled in the trolley with tea and juice.

'Well, with you busting a gut all day scrubbing down those fat patients of yours,' said Vandersteen, 'we thought we'd get out of your way and make life a bit easier for you.'

'If I didn't have to fill in a questionnaire the length of my arm for Mr Moustache out there, just so I can traipse in here like a sad old waitress to serve you a cup of tea, I'd be able to take on another job.'

'Sounds good to me,' said Vandersteen, 'you taking another job.'

'Is she like this with you, too?' said the nurse, looking around. Anna shook her head. I slunk back to bed.

'That one lost her tongue now, too?' she said to Vandersteen, waving her thumb over her shoulder at me.

Without so much as a nod or a wink to one another, all three of us maintained a unanimous silence.

'I've got a head like a potato, there's no other way to describe it,' said Anna, once night had fallen. 'A fat lump of a nose, pockmarks on my cheeks, thin lips, and a jaw like a Welsh scrum half. When you're a girl, it doesn't take you long to find out you're ugly. People tell you all the time, people you don't even know. They shout things at you while you're toddling down the aisle in the supermarket, while you're popping tomatoes into your shopping basket.'

I was sitting up in bed, my hands in my lap. Vandersteen was standing at the window.

'One thing's for sure, you won't be getting that face of

yours back,' said Vandersteen, trying to crank open the bottom section of the window.

'True, I won't get that face back,' said Anna. 'God's little joke.'

Vandersteen rammed the window with her shoulder and swore in pain.

'Now I get to miss the face I had,' said Anna. 'The way I used to be.'

'I don't know a single woman who thinks she's beautiful,' said Vandersteen. 'Not one.'

I searched for a smart reply that was nowhere to be found.

'And what's more,' said Vandersteen, sliding her reading glasses up the bridge of her nose and hunching over with her hands on her knees to size up the window's opening mechanism, 'when you're a woman it's second nature to weigh up what you really think against the effect you want to have on whoever you're talking to.'

'Second nature?' said Anna.

'Nothing odd about that,' Vandersteen continued. 'Perfectly normal. If you're a woman. But if I'm going to say what I really think, I see women do it all the time and it bugs the hell out of me.'

'If I'd been pretty it would have been worse,' said Anna. 'Still, ugly or pretty, the result's the same now, anyway.'

She straightened up her sheets.

'I read something in one of those daft magazines of Vandersteen's about how you're supposed to live in the moment. What a lot of rubbish. As if that means anything.'

There was a bang. Vandersteen had managed to get the window open.

'Yes, that's rubbish, all right,' she said in a pinched voice, her cheek pressed up against the glass. 'Living in the moment. We'd all be dogs if that was our natural state.'

With every ounce of her strength, Vandersteen strained to edge the window further open. Cigarette clamped tightly between her lips and clutching her lighter, she tried to squeeze her hand through the little gap. A curse rang out, and Vandersteen pulled back from the gap minus cigarette and lighter.

'Why can't these bloody windows open like bloody windows should? I mean, what's the point, otherwise?' said Vandersteen.

'I always used to carry a roll of black tape in my hand-bag,' said Anna. 'You know, the kind that tears off easily. Whenever I saw a poster of one of those supermodels, I'd tear a piece off and give her a Hitler moustache.'

'God, I'm gasping for a fag,' said Vandersteen. 'I'd set myself alight again if they'd let me smoke a ciggie first.'

'Is that your idea of a joke?' I said.

Vandersteen climbed back into bed.

'When it comes to looking death in the face, you can divide people into three categories,' she said. 'The ones that get angry, the ones that run, and the ones that freeze. Generally speaking, the runners are best off. I'm in the first category. I get angry. Not just angry, but livid. It's rarely the smart thing to do but I can't help myself. It's cost me dearly many a time. I could tell you a thing or two about what people will do to you, given half a chance. I don't have much weight to throw around, so when three bruisers are out to flatten you, the last thing you want to do is go for them. It's stupid. But I do it anyway. It's something I've had to learn to live with. I don't run away from trouble, I run toward it. So one day I decided I had to learn to fight better. Learn to fight smarter.'

'I've never had to fight,' I said.

'Don't you worry, Annie. You'll make a damn good soldier. I'll give you a shove in the direction of the trenches, if ever it's called for.'

I closed my eyes and wrapped my blanket tight around me.

'I had a boyfriend,' Anna said.

It was dark again, and everything was so much quieter than during the day.

'I don't know why I'm telling you this. Or, yes, perhaps I do. I'd be better off keeping my mouth shut.'

'Sometimes you just have to let it out, love,' said Vandersteen. 'What's his name?'

'Leendert,' Anna said.

'Nice name,' said Vandersteen. 'It's got a cosy ring to it.'

'I can't stop thinking about him,' said Anna. 'It's sinful.'

'Sinful?' said Vandersteen. 'Let's stop that kind of talk right here and now. You've done nothing wrong.'

'That's what you think,' said Anna.

'Yep, that's what I think.'

'What makes you think it's sinful, Anna?' I asked.

I stumbled for a second over my own name. I still had to get used to saying it to this girl in the bed across from me. Anna. It sounded so different, all of a sudden. It's like that with names, sometimes. Someone says, 'Who? Ralph? I don't know anyone called Ralph!' And then the other person says, 'Of course you do, he's this, that, and the other.' And then the first person says, 'Oh, you mean *Ralph*.' It's another name from another compartment.

'Is that what your parents think, too?' said Vandersteen.

'Maybe we're asking an awful lot of questions at once,' I said to Anna.

'I believe you have to save yourself. Till the right one comes along. But then... '

'Are you sure you want to talk about it?' I asked. 'You don't have to, you know.'

'What?' said Anna. 'How I ended up like this?'

'You don't have to,' I repeated, suddenly afraid I'd wind up having to answer the same question.

'My brother was born first. He was my parents' only child for years and years, and then, when no one expected it, along I came. It was a miracle, they said. After I was born, anyway. Beforehand, they were convinced I'd have Down's syndrome.'

'Are your parents still together?' asked Vandersteen.

'Where I come from, you don't get divorced,' said Anna. 'It's not an option.'

'That's helpful,' said Vandersteen.

'When we sat at the dinner table, my big brother Anton would always tell us about his day,' said Anna. 'Always. We all had to listen. What he had to say was interesting enough, but if he caught me drifting off, he'd slap me one. Once he attacked me with the fish slice and whacked me off my chair. Another time he pushed my face down into my dinner and held me there for what felt like ages. I nearly drowned in a plate of cabbage and mash.'

Anna gave a bitter laugh.

'No one said a word. It's bad manners not to pay attention, I know that. Of course I do. Anton was twenty when I was born, already a student. He'd sit at the table with his books and I had to sit next to him. He still lives at home, even though he's in his forties and doing very well for himself. Anton was my third parent. Maybe even my first. Anton is ever so smart and ever so charming. Everybody loves Anton.'

'I can't stand people like that,' said Vandersteen. 'People everybody loves.'

It was quiet for a moment.

'And he was the one who did this to me,' said Anna. 'That's why I didn't say a word to anyone. He mustn't ever find out where I am.'

'Damn right,' said Vandersteen.

'He's a detective and not just any old detective. He's way up there at the top of the ladder. He's told me before about the things he can get away with. The things he's done without anyone finding out. He's made people disappear, even beaten money out of them first. He has it all figured out. "Don't think for a second anyone will believe you if you're stupid enough to talk about what you know," he'd always say. "Everyone thinks the police force is a fine upstanding institution, a well-oiled machine, but that's not how things work." If there's one thing he's taught me, it's how easy it is to beat the system.'

Vandersteen and I began to splutter. Injustice is injustice. No one's above the law.

'You have to go to the police,' I said.

'And what about your parents?' fumed Vandersteen.

'Why haven't they done anything?'

'My parents couldn't care less about me. I wasn't much good at school and I wasn't a cute kid. I'm ugly. And they can't do anything. Or won't do anything. I'm not sure which. They must be scared, too.'

'Seriously, Anna,' I said, 'you need to report someone like that.'

'He thinks he's untouchable. When I think of the risks he's taken, it's frightening. If I had died, there would have been clues all over the place. Who knows, perhaps he had them all covered. Whatever happens, he mustn't find out where I am.'

Anna sighed.

'But he's bound to find out, one way or another. Or perhaps he already knows it's me, here in this hospital: the woman without a name. My guess is that I haven't been registered as a burns patient yet, and that Anton is hunting for people who have been admitted with burns. If anyone finds out what he's done, he stands to lose everything. But I'm too scared to talk. They won't believe me, anyway. They asked me all kinds of questions when they first brought me here. The police came to see me. I didn't say anything. Not a word. For days on end.'

'Tell your story to the copper at the door,' I said.

Anna glared at me.

'You just don't get it, do you?' she said. 'Didn't you hear what I said? I'm scared. I'll make a break for it soon. I'm getting better every day. Just a little while longer.'

I stared at the ceiling tiles.

'Sorry,' Anna said. 'I didn't mean to bite your head off. It's just that I have to get out of here. It's my only chance.'

'When you first mentioned your brother, I pictured one of those pasty-faced yokels,' said Vandersteen. 'The kind that knocks back cans of beer in a Portakabin and reeks of cheap deodorant.'

'I wish,' said Anna.

'What a nightmare,' said Vandersteen.

'And I'm still so ashamed,' said Anna.

'You have nothing to be ashamed of,' I said. 'Don't let anyone tell you otherwise. Not anyone. Ever.'

Anna picked at the skin on her face. Then she laid her pillow flat and slid under the covers. I wondered what she had been through, what he had done to her, but I didn't dare ask. Not just for Anna's sake, but for my own.

The next morning they let Anna look in the mirror for the first time.

'Are you sure?' asked the loud nurse.

Anna nodded. The nurse sat down beside her on the bed and placed a hand mirror face down on Anna's lap.

'Stupid bloody things,' the nurse said.

Anna picked up the mirror and turned it over. She jumped when she saw her face. Hurriedly she put the mirror back down on her lap and sat there for a moment with her eyes closed. The nurse put a hand on her arm. We watched as Anna timidly lifted the mirror again. To us she looked like Anna. She looked like herself.

'So you come from a long line of God-fearing Christians,' said Vandersteen, when we were alone again.

'I still like to pray,' said Anna. 'That has nothing much to do with my upbringing.'

'I think it's a lovely ritual,' I said. 'Giving thanks for the food on your table.'

'I've got to hand it to you, Annie, you're a walking cliché,' said Vandersteen.

'Well, it is, isn't it?' I said.

'I bet you're one of those lapsed Catholics,' she said. 'Can't wait to go flouncing down the aisle on your wedding day, but the only time you ever set foot in a church is when someone's snuffed it.'

'And what makes you think I'm Catholic?'

'Only a lapsed Catholic would say, "Oooh, it's a lovely ritual" in the middle of a conversation about what someone actually believes in.'

She was right, damn her. I did get married in church for the sake of the ritual. I clenched my fist. Vandersteen and her bloody sixth sense.

'I have nothing to do with the church,' I said.

'I don't believe a word of it,' Vandersteen said.

'That's just the problem,' said Anna.

'You're the type that only calls out to God when she's in trouble,' Vandersteen went on at me. 'When everything's hunky-dory it's all your own doing. Am I right?'

I didn't say anything.

'Silence is consent,' said Vandersteen.

'Is not,' I said.

Anna's faith in God had nothing to do with what had happened to her. It had everything to do with the God-fearing folk around her. I wasn't lying in a hospital bed because of something that had happened to me, something beyond my control. I was lying here because it was my own fault. If only I had... If only I could... If only that hadn't happened, then… I could come up with a mitigating circumstance or two. But that would only make it worse. I know the truth. That's the worst of it: the knowing. There are no mitigating circumstances.

'I have a dyslexic heart,' I said.

'A what?' said Anna.

'A dyslexic heart,' I said. 'I can feel things, and everyone's explained them to me time and time again, but somehow I can't seem to get it all to make sense.'

'Yes,' said Anna. 'I know what you mean.'

'And the thing is, since I've been here in this room, it hasn't been nearly as bad,' I said.

'That's because all three of us have a dyslexic heart,' said Vandersteen.

I felt a warm surge inside me. In the place where the knot usually is. That exact spot.

'Looks like we're a club,' I said. 'The dyslexic hearts club.'

My heart gave a little jump for joy.

'And believe me, I'm not one for clubs,' I said.

'No,' said Anna. 'None of us are.'

'The dyslexic hearts club,' said Vandersteen. 'Perhaps that brother of yours should start looking for us in the cardiac unit.'

That night I was woken up by Vandersteen. She was over by the window again.

'What are you up to?' I said.

Anna was sleeping.

'Dropped your lighter out the window again?'

'I don't know what it is. I'm feeling restless. And now that car's there again.'

I hauled myself out of bed and padded over to where she was standing.

'Look,' she said, pointing at a parked car down below. Inside, the lights were on and cigarette smoke curled from an open window.

'It was there last night, too. I'm sure of it.'

'Must be someone working night shift,' I said. 'Or over at casualty.'

'Nope,' said Vandersteen. 'Wrong car park. This one's visitors only.'

She was right. There were only one or two cars parked down below. The staff car park along the way was chock-a-block.

'Perhaps someone's dying and they're holding a vigil?'

Vandersteen rubbed the glass with a bony finger, as if she had the power to erase the car. Anna's bedclothes rustled.

'Two nights in a row,' said Vandersteen. 'Same car, same spot.'

We peered down at the miniature landscape beneath us.

Two men emerged from the night entrance and strolled across to the car. They got in and it drove off.

'See. It's a vigil,' I said.

'All right,' said Vandersteen.

We stood there for a while and then crept back into bed. Sleep was a long time coming.

Slowly but surely we became nocturnal. It meant we could talk more or less uninterrupted. Work only came up once in our hospital conversations. It all began when Vandersteen asked Anna what she did for a living. Anna said she worked in home care, and that she was taking a course.

'Do you enjoy that?' asked Vandersteen. 'Going to school?'

Anna shrugged.

'I like the work,' she said.

'I always thought everything would change, once I got to secondary school,' said Vandersteen. 'And then I thought everything would get better once I became a student. But even when I started work, everything stayed the same.'

'Stayed the same how?' I asked.

'The law of the jungle. The pecking order. Dog eat dog.'

'Do you have any comparisons that don't involve animals?' I asked.

'No,' said Vandersteen. 'We're all just muddling along. That's why conspiracy theories are rubbish. People swear blind that there's some big master plan, that the people at the top know what they're doing. But they don't—that's the terrifying thing. The powers that be don't have a plan, either. We're stuck in the school playground forever.'

'Well done,' I said. 'Not a single animal reference.'

'See,' said Vandersteen. 'You *can* teach an old dog... Oh, bugger!'

'What kind of work do you do?' Anna asked me.

'I work at an office,' I said.

I tried to imagine a day at the open-plan taxidermy office: skinning animals, cleaning skins, disposing of the animals' organs. I pictured myself working away at a desk, rolling across a sea of grey carpet tiles in my office chair, and yelling 'Nearly weekend!' on a Wednesday to the delight of my co-workers. Fact was, I worked away in splendid isolation at my own workbench on the boat. While Nelis headed out to the office five days a week, I drank coffee in my own kitchen, ate lunch at my own table, and when I was working I skinned the animals people brought to my door. I had a good reputation, if I say so myself. I made a decent living, too. Fame is never all it's cracked up to be, of course. But in my own line of work I felt I had something to be proud of.

'And?' said Vandersteen. 'Do you work according to a plan?'

'No,' I said.

I had no idea how an office was organized.

'Ha!' said Vandersteen. 'What did I tell you? We kid ourselves on that we're beavering away in an ant colony, but it's dog eat dog all the while.'

The next night, Vandersteen slid open the drawer of her bedside table and produced another cigarette. She shuffled over to the window and started cranking the handle.

'Where on Earth do you keep getting those cigarettes from?' asked Anna.

'I nick 'em off the loud nurse. Along with… a pair of tweezers. Snatched them off the trolley and tucked them down the back of my knickers. My right arse cheek must look like a three-year-old's Etch-A-Sketch by now. Laying hands on another lighter was an adventure in its own right. But if it's all the same to you, I'd like to finally avail myself of the chance to have a fag on the fly. It's got to the stage where I can't even think straight. And one cigarette never killed anyone, now did it?'

Vandersteen let out a wheezy laugh, took her cigarette between the tweezers, and stuck her hand through the narrow gap in the window. Then she wormed the lighter through the gap with her other hand. There was just enough space.

'Well, what do you know… '

The end of the cigarette began to glow faintly.

'Have you got a whole pack?' Anna asked.

'Keep it down a sec, Tubs,' said Vandersteen.

Vandersteen extricated the hand that held the lighter, craned her neck into the gap and pouted her lips as far as they would go. Trembling with anticipation, the hand that held the tweezers that held the cigarette crept closer to her mouth. Anna and I were on the edge of our beds. It was like watching a World Cup final with Vandersteen stepping up to take the deciding penalty. As the filter came closer and closer to her mouth, she started to make little sucking motions. Just as her lips were about to kiss the filter, the faint glow at the end of the cigarette died. She straightened up.

'Fuckety-fuck-fuck,' she said.

'Language!' said Anna.

Vandersteen gave it another go, but she'd lost her momentum. The cigarette fell, the lighter fell, and with only the tweezers to cling to, Vandersteen stared forlornly out the window.

'There's that car again,' she said.

I slid out of bed. Sparks flew as someone fired a burning fag end out of one of the car windows. Poor old Vandersteen. Everyone in the whole wide world was puffing away to their heart's content while she was locked up in here, barely hanging on. Anna pulled the covers up snug around her and turned her back to us. I went over and sat on the edge of her bed.

'Let me see what I can find out from our pal at the door,' I said.

'No,' Anna hissed.

'I won't say anything about you,' I said. 'Scouts' honour. I'll just act the concerned female. I can pull that off easily enough.'

Vandersteen nodded her approval.

I went over and opened the door. The copper jumped and looked up from his magazine. *Popular Science*. He had bags under his eyes and a plastic cup full of coffee was steaming at his side. The corridor was deserted.

'Do you mind if I ask you something?' I said.

My voice echoed down the corridor. The copper shifted in his seat and scratched the black stubble on his cheek. It made a rasping sound.

'Well?' he asked.

'Perhaps I'm fretting about nothing, but I couldn't help noticing that for the past three nights the same car has been parked out there in the car park. It stays there half the night.'

'Is that right?' said the copper, without changing his expression.

'Yes,' I said. 'I think there's something fishy going on.'

The copper put down *Popular Science* and picked up the cup from the little table next to him.

'And how would you know it's parked there half the night? Are you parked at the window half the night, too?'

'Vandersteen has trouble sleeping,' I said.

The copper gave me a long, hard look and then took a sip of his coffee.

'Oh,' he said. 'Sorry to hear it.'

His free hand was already reaching for *Popular Science* again. I smelled the coffee and heard Vandersteen coming up behind me. The copper put down his plastic cup. I crossed my arms.

'Tell you what,' he said. 'Why don't you give the night nurse a beep, or whatever it is you have to do to get attention in there.'

He stretched out his arm and pushed gently against my leg. I took a step back and bumped into Vandersteen. The copper leaned forward and peered into the room, pulling a face like he was fishing for turds in a bagful of snakes. The legs of his chair made a scraping sound as he hooked a finger around the handle and pulled the door shut.

'He told us to press the button,' I said.

'We're *not* going to press the button,' said Anna.

Down in the car park the men were piling back into the car.

'Do any of them look familiar?' I asked.

'Anton has rules. One of them is that he doesn't clean up this kind of mess in person.'

The car drove off.

'Do you think they've been able to discover anything?' I said.

'He often talks about work at the dinner table,' said Anna. 'It's like he's giving a lecture. About how stupid most people are. How easy it is to track them down. He's a good detective.'

Because Vandersteen insisted on knowing once and for all what had happened to Anna, she told us about the night when Anton dragged her out of bed.

'Before I knew what was happening, I was lying in the corner of my bedroom, trussed up with tie wraps, my nose pressed against the grubby rug under the radiator. I remember the smell exactly: dust, socks, and shoes. Like a school gym. Then Anton plastered duct tape over my mouth and wrapped me in a carpet.'

Tie wraps and duct tape, I thought. Uninvent tie wraps and duct tape, and the whole world would fall apart.

'Once I'd been bundled into the boot of the car, I tried to think. There were two choices: beg or yell. I yelled. Nothing happened. In panic I felt along the edges of the boot for a button or a handle. Isn't there some kind of law that you have to be able to open a car boot from the inside? Or is that only trucks? Anton had found out I had a thing with Leendert.'

There was no handle on the inside of the car boot. She tried to reach one of the tail lights, picking away at the lining with her nails till the fitting came loose and the lamp fell inward. She pulled it clear and stuck her fingers into the gap to push out the red plastic casing. Her knuckles began to bleed, but eventually she managed it. The red plastic shot out and bounced off the tarmac and into the verge.

'I tried to use the lamp to signal through the hole I'd made. I thought someone would be bound to notice a strange light moving around where the tail light should be. The car stopped. I felt the door slam, and suddenly Anton's face appeared at the hole. I could see his eye, right up close. He blinked once. Then the boot opened and he thumped me hard in the face. I saw his fist coming at me again, and everything went black.'

A while later she woke up in the dark. She could hear the sound of running water. At least she thought it was water. It wasn't. You can't use water to set fire to a shed.

'It didn't take me long to realize I was lying in a shed, and that Anton was outside, sloshing petrol against the walls. The wood caught fire. I could see the flames licking the cracks between the planks, shooting up to the roof. I heard Anton shout "Whore!" I could barely move. I lay there squirming inside that carpet. It was getting hotter and the smoke was getting thicker. I tried to shout, but all I could do was cough.'

Then Anna fell silent.

'Oh, Tubby,' said Vandersteen.

'And my hair,' Anna sobbed. 'All my beautiful hair is gone. It was the only thing I was proud of, and now that's gone, too. I have nothing left. Nothing.'

She cried gentle, restrained tears. It was too dark to tell whether Vandersteen was crying, too. I wasn't, but God knows I wanted to.

'I'm glad you're here,' Vandersteen whispered. 'Here with us.'

'Yes,' said Anna.

Yes, I thought, too. Thank goodness you're here. It was then that I decided I could never tell them what I had done. Arson. Revenge. It was all too close for comfort. Sudden knowledge can change the course of any story.

Vandersteen slipped gently out of Anna's embrace and off her bed. She went over to her own bed and took something out of her drawer. Then she walked over to the mirrorless bathroom and clicked on the tube light above the washbasin. I squinted in the bright light that came from the open door.

'What are you doing?' I heard Anna ask. She was answered by the buzz of a trimmer mowing through hair.

Anna stumbled over to the bathroom.

'What on Earth are you doing?' she asked again, her voice louder now.

'One for all, all for one,' said Vandersteen.

'No! You can't!' Anna cried.

'Not so loud!' I hissed, as I reached the bathroom doorway.

'Yes, I can,' Vandersteen whispered to Anna. 'So that's enough of your lip. I'll do what I want to do.'

Thick tufts of long black-grey hair fell into the washbasin. Vandersteen turned and her eyes met mine.

'Where did you get that trimmer?' I whispered.

'Added bonus when I was making my play for the tweezers.'

'Let me have it when you're finished, will you?' I said.

When the basin was full of hair, she handed me the trimmer. Fifteen minutes later, we were all as bald as a coot. I ran my hand over my head. It felt soft and fuzzy.

When I woke up the next morning, the grouchy nurse was already in the room.

'If I don't have a smoke soon, I'll *die*,' I heard Vandersteen say.

'You've all taken leave of your senses,' said the nurse.

She turned to me. 'I suppose the Yul Brynner look was your idea? If I've said it once, I've said it a hundred times. Two hardened criminals and a mystery mute in one room is asking for trouble.'

That's when it all went wrong.

'Fuck!' said Vandersteen, as she tried to light another cigarette through the gap in the open window.

'Was that your last one?' I said.

'It's that car again.'

Vandersteen pressed a finger to the glass.

'Anna,' she said. 'Come here a sec.'

Anna went to the window and gasped. She thought she recognized one of the men.

'What do we do now?' said Anna. She had gone back to sit on her bed, and was kneading a corner of her blanket.

'No need to panic,' said Vandersteen.

'We have to get out of here,' said Anna.

I pressed the button to call the nurses, then marched over to the door and yanked it open. The copper looked up.

'Something's wrong,' I said.

'Oh,' said the copper.

He didn't move a muscle.

'You really do have to do something, this time,' I said. 'I've already pressed the button.'

We looked down the corridor. It was empty and silent.

'Fair enough,' said the copper. 'We'll wait.'

The empty corridor stayed that way.

Anna and Vandersteen came and stood behind me.

'What's keeping the nurses?'

'I don't know,' said the copper.

He looked each of us up and down in turn, and then shifted in his chair. A tube light at the end of the corridor flickered.

Then, from somewhere in the building, we heard a scream.

Suddenly the copper was wide awake, his face completely transformed. I couldn't stop staring at it. It was as if a younger, fitter nephew had taken possession of his body. Vandersteen took my arm and I jumped.

'Time to go,' she said.

The copper was on his feet and peering down the corridor.

'You're not going anywhere,' he said, waving us back into the room.

He put one hand on his holster. Vandersteen pressed the button again.

'Don't,' said Anna.

The copper gawped at her like he'd heard a voice from on high.

'Well, I never,' he said.

'No one's coming,' said Vandersteen.

We heard another scream, immediately followed by a loud bang. The copper sprinted down the corridor, grabbed the walkie-talkie on his sleeve and shouted into it.

'Everyone stays put,' he barked at us. 'No one wanders off without me. We're not going to move now.'

'Speak for yourself,' said Vandersteen. She ran over and punched the copper square in the face.

'What the hell are you doing?' I shouted.

Vandersteen looked at her fist in surprise.

'God knows where that came from,' she said, rubbing her knuckles.

'Jesus,' cried the copper, putting his hand to his nose and sounding like he was bunged up with a cold. Blood began seeping through his fingers.

'Cheeshush,' he said again.

With his free hand, the copper tugged Vandersteen by the collar and tried to force her down onto the floor. He had no idea what he was getting into. No sooner had he grabbed her than she pounced onto his back. Anna and I screamed at them to stop. The copper began to flail around and blood flew everywhere as we tried to separate them. The copper managed to shake free, took a few steps back, and drew his gun. Anna skidded part-way down the corridor on her back and I held on tight to Vandersteen.

'Back inside,' panted the copper, pointing to our room.

With Vandersteen still in my arms, I took a couple of steps back, and eased her onto her feet.

'Who's the enemy around here?' I said to the copper.

'That's what I was wondering,' he said.

He began yelling into his walkie-talkie again, hurried and tense.

Anna scrambled to her feet and came and stood behind me.

'Why is no one coming?' she asked.

'This is bad,' said the copper.

His walkie-talkie squealed and his nose continued to bleed. Anna handed him a tissue from the bathroom. He barked another code into his mouthpiece. Something about a gunshot. Something about backup. Down the corridor, the light flickered again.

'Get back inside,' growled the copper again, waving his gun at us. We did as we were told.

'We have to get out of here,' said Vandersteen, through clenched teeth. 'Now.'

'Yes,' I said. 'Or do any of us feel like waiting for back-up?'

Anna shook her head. We looked at the copper as he scanned the corridor for signs of life. His walkie-talkie squealed again.

'Listen, mister,' said Vandersteen. 'We're making a run for it. Now. You can join us if you like.'

The copper screamed at us not to go anywhere. Anna sank onto her bed and I ran to the window. The car park below was deserted. From the corridor I could hear the copper and Vandersteen shouting at each other, then came a thump and a groan. I ran out and jumped on the thrashing tangle of arms and legs that was the two of them. They were wrestling for the gun. Anna rushed to the doorway and looked on anxiously. Vandersteen was trying her darnedest to overpower the copper, and I was trying to pry her loose. Bang! I fell against the wall and Vandersteen rolled off the copper. He lay on the floor, still clutching the gun. I laid my hand on his heaving chest. A slow red stain spread across his belly. Vander-steen grabbed me by the arm. The copper moaned.

'Run!' she hollered.

The three of us pelted down the corridor in our night-clothes. The notepad on my bedside table flashed into my mind and then was gone. Without slowing down, I looked around at the copper. I'm sorry, I thought. I'm so very sorry.

We had almost reached the end of the corridor when Vandersteen nearly stopped in her tracks. Through the window of the nurses' station we saw three armed men, guns pointed at two hunched figures with bags over their heads. One of the gunmen was flicking through papers in a ring binder. Another was shouting at the two hostages. The third man spotted us and leaped up. In a split second, Vandersteen changed course and bolted down a corridor to the left, pulling Anna behind her by the sleeve. I followed. Anna was breathing heavily.

'There's a service lift up ahead somewhere,' yelled Vandersteen.

We dived around the corner. I caught up with Vandersteen, and Anna stumbled along behind us.

'I couldn't do anything to stop it,' I gasped. 'I couldn't do anything.'

'It's okay,' Vandersteen wheezed. 'Now shut up and run.'

I called out to God but He wasn't born yesterday. He wasn't about to pull out all the stops for someone who'd reduced Him to a lovely ritual.

Vandersteen raced on ahead of us on her spindly legs, looking like a stork struggling to take flight. My back was soaking with sweat. I had no idea how she was able to keep up this pace after all those weeks confined to bed.

'Left!' Vandersteen shouted.

The sign above the open doors read 'Service lift. Authorized personnel only.'

We piled in.

'Basement!'

Vandersteen put her hands on her knees and puffed. I hit the button. One thousand times I hit the button for the underground car park. The lift juddered and began to descend. I was panting like an old dog at the height of summer. We all were. Panting and speechless. It was as if someone had hit pause on a computer game. Then the lift doors opened and we were off again.

I inhaled the smell of petrol.

Using a length of wire she'd stripped from the lining of a wheelchair next to the lift, Vandersteen was trying to pick the lock of a dinky little hatchback in a dim corner of the vast hospital basement.

'Get a move on,' I said.

Lost in concentration, Vandersteen stared off into the distance, making intricate movements with the wire in her hands. The door clicked open.

'We're not there yet,' she said.

She climbed into the car. I slid into the passenger seat, and Anna threw herself in the back. Vandersteen ripped off the plastic casing under the steering wheel and began to fiddle with the wires. The engine sprang into life.

'Bingo,' she said. 'Like riding a bike.'

Anna was slumped against the window. Vandersteen took off, tyres screeching. I leaned into every turn. Turn after turn through the cavernous underground space, convinced the little hatchback was going to tip over at any moment. Red turned to green and a garage door began to roll up slowly. Vandersteen slammed her foot down, and we were all thrown back in our seats. A uniformed security guard leaped out of the way. The roof of the car grazed the bottom of the door, and suddenly we were out in the open air, as if we'd been shot from a cannon.

'Wind down the window!' yelled Vandersteen. 'Anna! Wind down the window!'

I wound the window down, and for the first time in God knows how long, I felt the wind on my face. I closed my eyes.

We swung onto the road, a dual carriageway flanked by fields of cows. A layer of mist hung over the grass. The hospital was rapidly shrinking away to nothing in the wing mirror. Anna had turned around and was staring out the rear window.

'They're after us,' she said.

In the mirror I could see them, too. Headlights approaching, travelling faster than we were. Way too fast.

'Full throttle,' I shouted.

'My foot's already halfway through the floor,' Vandersteen yelled back.

I saw her right leg cramping under the strain of pushing harder on a pedal that had nowhere else to go. Road signs announced a motorway access ramp up ahead. Vandersteen glanced over her shoulder.

'Okay,' she said. 'Hold onto yer hats. Here we go.'

She began to sing and in the midst of all the panic, I recognized it as the song of the Singing Nun.

'*Dominique, nique, nique, s'en allait tout simplement, routier pauvre et chantant. En tous chemins, en tous lieux, il ne parle que du bon Dieu. Il ne parle que du bon Dieu.'*

On the *D* of the final 'Dieu' she slammed on the brakes and yanked on the steering wheel. I clung to the grip above the door and screamed like I'd never screamed before. Twin sirens: Anna's voice and mine, wailing in unison.

'Not much point holding onto the car that's knocking you about!' Vandersteen yelled.

We skidded onto the other lane and shot past our pursuers in the opposite direction. I turned to see them slamming on the brakes, too. I couldn't make out the men in the car, only that there were three of them.

'Is he in the car?' I asked Anna.

Anna didn't answer.

'This would be so much better in a stick shift,' said Vandersteen, gritting her teeth.

She kept on singing, gave the steering wheel another tug, and sped over the hard shoulder against the flow of the oncoming traffic and onto the motorway.

'*Certain jour un hérétique. Par des ronces le conduit. Mais notre père, Dominique, par sa joie le convertit.'*

A truck flashed its lights, swerved to avoid us, and thundered past, blasting its horn at us as we tore along in the wrong direction. The automatic transmission squealed like an old vacuum cleaner with a sock stuck in the nozzle. I could see them gaining on us down the hard shoulder. Vandersteen kept on humming her little French song. The oncoming cars and trucks blurred into a pulsating beam of blinding headlights, accompanied by a nuns' choir of horns in Doppler effect. I felt sick. Anna lay motionless on the back seat. Vandersteen tried every insane manoeuvre she could think of to shake off our pursuers. We veered off and drove into a wood. I could not believe we would ever be safe again.

The hatchback was parked in a clump of bushes. Pale morning light filtered through the leaves and the steamed-up windows. Everything felt damp. I could hear Anna's laboured breathing from the back seat. I turned and placed a hand on her quivering shoulder. Vandersteen had fallen asleep as soon as she'd parked the car, and was snoring heavily. The cold had long since seeped through my hospital pyjamas.

'It'll be all right,' I said. 'We'll drive to a police station and explain everything. It's time we took that chance. They can't just ignore us.'

'Okay,' said Anna, with a lump in her throat.

'Good,' I said.

I poked Vandersteen. She sat bolt upright with a yelp and blew her nose on the sleeve of her nightgown.

'So,' she said. 'Shall we?'

Anna nodded. Gingerly, Vandersteen reversed the hatchback out of the bushes. It was still misty. She left the lights off.

'They must've given up,' I said.

'Yes,' said Vandersteen. 'Even gangsters have a job to go to.'

Vandersteen turned onto a country road and switched the lights on. There was a fair bit of traffic.

Before we knew it, we were caught up in the rush hour.

'Shit,' said Vandersteen.

She tapped the dials on the dashboard.

'I hope we've got enough in the tank to make it.'

'If you want to disappear off the face of the Earth, you need to plan it at least three months in advance,' said Anna. 'You can't just run away. And you need to stay off the motorways.'

She stared blankly out the window. Every now and again her mouth twitched. I turned on the radio. House music blared and thudded through the car. Vandersteen swore and gave the dial a spin. A man's voice began to speak. I turned the volume down.

'We have Mr Dubois on the line, spokesman for the hospital where the hostage drama took place. Mr Dubois, can you tell us anything about the condition of the victims?'

I turned the volume back up.

Mr Dubois explained that two nurses had been admitted to hospital for observation. Brute force had been used. He mentioned firearms, and the bags that had been put over the nurses' heads.

'A police officer was shot with his own weapon. He is currently under sedation. His condition is critical.'

'The three suspects fled the scene in a stolen car,' said the presenter.

'Fuckers,' said Vandersteen.

'Can you tell us why none of the adjacent wards were warned? Why no one raised the alarm even after shots were fired? How could this have been allowed to happen?'

'All these matters will be addressed in the thorough investigation we have now launched,' said the spokesman.

'We now know the police were at the scene while the

three assailants were still in the building. Can you explain why they only came to the aid of the victims thirty minutes after these criminals had made their getaway?'

'That is a question for the police. As I am sure you understand, we are not privy to the workings of their internal procedures.'

'I wondered about that myself,' I said.

'Quiet!' Vandersteen snapped.

'As no such information has been made available to us, I am simply unable to answer that question at this juncture.'

'Can you confirm reports that the hospital's communication system has been in need of a major overhaul for some time?'

'As I have already said,' said the spokesman, irked, 'we have launched a thorough investigation and you can rest assured that no stone will... '

'The three fugitives were being held together in the same room, a room intended for two patients. Two of the three were under detention or awaiting trial. Surely that is asking for trouble, Mr Dubois? Three criminals in one room?'

'What the... ?' shouted Vandersteen.

'So now they think we... ?' said Anna.

I cranked up the volume again.

'It would appear that administrative errors were made regarding the accommodation of our clients. All three had to be placed under surveillance, and our system did not cater for this as effectively as it might have. An unfortunate turn of events. And let me make it clear that the description "three criminals" is yours, not mine.'

'The three fugitives are known to the police: three ruthless, trigger-happy criminals. This case is being taken very seriously indeed.'

'It is not my place to comment. That, too, is a matter for the police, though we will, of course, be lending our fullest cooperation throughout the investigation.'

The presenter brought the interview to a close and a cheery tune began to play. I'm not one to use a word like 'gobsmacked'. I'd happily smack the gob of anyone who does. But it was the only word to describe that moment. There we sat, gobs well and truly smacked, staring into space.

Vandersteen clicked on the indicator and turned off down a country lane. We parked in the cover of another patch of woodland. When the song was over, Vandersteen turned up the radio again. More news just in about the fugitives. We had been identified as Anna van Veen and Anna Vandersteen. The hospital had been unable to provide information on the identity of the third person.

'She was simply known as "Ms X." Can you tell us any more about this mysterious third woman?'

Mr Dubois dodged the question, and the presenter segued into another news item. We gazed out at the leaves. Lost in thought, Vandersteen chewed on her thumbnail. Rain began to fall.

'So your name's Anna, too?' I asked, after a while.

'Of course not,' said Vandersteen. 'What a crock of shit. That hospital couldn't organize its way out of a paper bag. They're making it up as they go along. According to their records, everyone's called Anna. Except this one here in the back seat. Our very own Ms X.'

The stable was cold but dry. I was sitting in the hay with Anna, looking on as Vandersteen paced up and down between two sheep.

'She needs a cigarette,' said Anna.

'Is that what it is?' I said.

'I hope so,' Anna replied.

One of the sheep bleated. The other sheep bleated back.

'Can everyone just shut the fuck up?' yelled Vandersteen. 'I'm trying to think, here.'

The first sheep snorted.

'You, too, sunshine,' said Vandersteen. She poked the sheep in the face with a bony finger. 'Zip your mangy gob.'

The sheep blinked and pulled its head back. Bending at the knee it lay down, staring huffily into the corner with its front legs crossed.

'That's more like it,' said Vandersteen.

We had pushed the hatchback into a tangle of rhododendrons and walked deeper into the woods. It was cold and wet. Typical Dutch drizzle. Not even honest-to-goodness rain, just a plant-sprayer on repeat. It wasn't much better here in the hay, but Anna was nice and warm. I snuggled up against her.

'Do you mind?' I asked.

'No, it's fine,' Anna said.

She put her arm around me.

'Right, then,' said Vandersteen, stroking the other sheep's head. 'What's our next move? The dyslexic hearts club have nothing. Nada. No cigarettes, nothing.'

By this time, hunger was starting to set in.

'So, top priority is to get ourselves something,' said Vandersteen. 'Cigarettes, of course, and... '

Every now and then I felt Anna's tummy rumble. With my head on her chest, it came through loud and clear.

'And money. And clothes,' said Vandersteen. 'Maybe get ourselves another car. Something along those lines. And then there's the delicate matter of how many coppers we've got chasing us.'

Vandersteen had a think. She squatted down in front of the second sheep.

'What would you do, darlin'?'

The sheep was clearly in two minds.

'If it turns out she can talk with the animals, it'll be the end of me,' Anna whispered in my ear.

Vandersteen stood up with a jerk, sucking in an extraordinary amount of air through her nose.

'I propose,' said Vandersteen, 'that we break in somewhere. In broad daylight, while everyone's out at work. There must be a house around here somewhere.'

The sheep bleated in agreement.

'It's just as well we didn't steal a truck,' said Vandersteen, as she settled down in the hay with us. 'We'd never have been able to hide that in the bushes. Though I wouldn't say no to stealing a truck. Just for the hell of it.'

The rain pattered on the roof of the stable, and Anna made herself comfortable in the hay. We huddled together.

'You're always so nice and warm,' I said, as I nodded off to sleep. 'I always used to say to my husband: one of your finest qualities is that you're so toasty.'

'I thought you didn't have a husband?'

'Oh, right,' I said.

Vandersteen rustled among the hay.

'You said you wanted nothing to do with love.'

'Yes... eh... no,' I stammered.

I took a deep breath. In, out.

'He cheated on me.'

Anna looked at me.

'That wasn't the deal,' she said. 'You weren't supposed to lie.'

'No,' I said.

'And where's this husband of yours now?' asked Vandersteen.

'Dead,' I said.

'Hmm,' said Vandersteen.

I nodded.

'How did he die?' asked Anna.

'I killed him,' I said.

'So that was it,' said Vandersteen.

'Yes, that was it,' I said.

'Nice to know you're even further up shit creek than I am,' said Vandersteen.

My parents had a holiday cottage on an island, a cottage at the edge of a wood. A little wooden house with blue shutters. No electricity, no running water. Instead we had a fireplace, a kitchen with a wood-burning stove, and a well in the back garden. We used our bathwater to flush the toilet. There was a shed in the back garden, too, and we grew runner beans, cabbages, and Brussels sprouts in neat little rows. The wood was home to chickens that had once belonged to someone. I used to feed them at the weekend when no one was looking. Every Friday we got in the car and headed for the island. We parked on the quay and took the ferry across. Once or twice a year we would join a group of walkers and make the five-hour crossing on foot, over the mudflats from the quay to our house on the island, with sturdy boots, backpacks, and a guide to lead the way. We slept under the roof of our island cottage, climbing up to bed on a set of wobbly wooden steps at one end of the living room. I slept in one corner and my parents in the other. We didn't talk much. We ate, we cycled, we read. On the island, life went on as usual.

I grew up in a tenement flat in a medium-sized town where no runner beans grew and no chickens scratched around. That was fine with me. I had my own room and it was only a short walk to school. At primary school there was a boy in my class who was taken away by another teacher once a week to practise reading and writing. I never really understood why.

I used to daydream. I would think up a story and stick to it as long as I could, until I began to get bored, and then I'd dream up a new one. I can still remember them clearly. As if they really happened. They were how things were supposed to be. I never found anything in real life that gave me that feeling, ever. Not till I wound up in hospital with Anna and Vandersteen.

The first bird I ever stuffed was Hetty. She was one of the woodland chickens that used to scratch around outside our wooden cottage. We were friends, the chicken and I. It was a new spring day, the day I first noticed her. There was a smell in the air that said winter was over. I was wandering around the fringes of the woods in search of nettles, sorrel, and shepherd's purse for the pot of soup I was planning to boil up over a campfire behind the shed. I had a piece of French bread and a stock cube in my pocket. Hetty sat there looking at me. If she'd been human, she'd have had her arms and legs crossed.

'Where did all your little friends go?' I asked.

She didn't reply. I flopped down next to her on the moss, but she didn't budge. When I put my hand on her back and stroked her gently, she clucked long and low. We polished off the bread together. I never did get around to making soup that day.

Then one day she was dead. I found her lying under a bush next to the cottage. I can still remember standing there with Hetty in my arms, feeling lost and looking around helplessly because I couldn't believe she had up and died on me. I pressed my little friend to my chest and stood there for a while, imagining I was a superhero with special bird-saving powers, that I could bring her back to life. If you want something badly enough, it will happen. That's another one of those things people like to say. Slowly, Hetty grew colder and stiffer. I took her inside with me.

'What have you got there?' asked my father.

'Hetty,' I said.

'For God's sake, throw that thing away,' said my mother.

My father tried to take Hetty out of my arms, but I wouldn't let go.

'I don't want to throw her away,' I said. 'That's not nice. I want to keep her.'

'It's dead! Bury it!' said my mother.

My father made another attempt to take the bird from my arms, but I turned my back on him. I stood with my nose to wall, holding on tight to Hetty.

'So you really want to keep her?'

I nodded.

'I know what we can do,' he said.

My mother raised a hand to her forehead.

'Trust me,' said my father. 'Scouts' honour.'

My father sat me on the back of his bike. I held Hetty close as he pedalled over to the village. We knocked on the door of a crooked little house and a little old pointy-faced man opened the door. My father nodded at Hetty and explained what had happened. The man looked at me. I nodded sadly.

'And you don't just want to bury the bird?' he said. 'That's what people do when a pet dies.'

'Don't you stuff and mount pets?' my father asked.

'I only stuff trophies.'

He looked sour-faced at the chicken in my arms.

'She *is* a trophy,' I said.

The man stepped aside and let us in. He allowed us to stand next to him at his bench and watch him work. By the time we got back to the cottage, it was already time to eat, pack, and catch the next ferry home. We would be able to collect Hetty the following weekend.

'Remember, this means you won't be getting a birthday present this year,' my father said.

At the library I read everything I could find about the art of preparing, stuffing, and mounting animals. I was especially interested in birds because of Hetty. I always kept her beside my bed, and later, when Nelis and I had bought the houseboat, she proudly kept watch on the sideboard next to the easy chair in my room. The perfect pet. I feel something close to heartache when I think of her lying at the bottom of the harbour along with all the other birds. That hurts as much as everything else put together. Strange, how the pain of everything else can't outweigh the pain of one dead bird. Everything else. My husband. All those people.

We lay on a grassy hillock looking down at a rustic farmhouse a short distance away.

'The burning question is,' said Vandersteen, 'are we looking at a real farm, or one that's been tarted up by a couple of baby boomers or double-income hipsters? Hipsters is my guess. Real farmers don't go in for fancy trim. But if they're too hip, they'll have an alarm to protect their designer goodies. Oh well. The good Lord loves a trier. Or is it a liar? I can never remember.'

'The good Lord loves a sinner,' I said.

'That'll do me,' said Vandersteen.

She scampered down to the farmhouse, looking like a ghost or a white witch, her nightgown flapping around her. We saw her creep around the farmhouse and climb up onto the roof at the back. Then she vanished.

When Vandersteen reappeared, we barely recognized her. With three giant backpacks slung over her shoulders, she came charging up the hill like the devil was after her.

'Hipsters!' she panted as she ran toward us. 'Come on! Get up and run.'

'Hip, but not too hip,' said Vandersteen, as she flopped down on the grass. I was leaning against a tree. Anna came staggering up behind us.

'I've had tougher jobs,' said Vandersteen. 'I was able to get in through that window on the roof. Found some cash stashed in an old tin in the kitchen.'

'If you want to disappear off the face of the Earth, never pay with plastic,' said Anna.

'Everyone hides their money in an old tin. Or in a book. You get a lot of that, too. One with "love" in the title. Never fails.'

Vandersteen rooted around in one of the backpacks and triumphantly produced a pouch of tobacco. She punched the air and immediately began to roll a cigarette, holding the flame to it with the devotion of an altar boy who's been allowed to light the first advent candle. She inhaled long and deep.

'Aaaah,' she said.

We looked on in rapt attention as Vandersteen communed with her cigarette.

'First things first. Time for a makeover, so we can get a bite to eat like decent folk.'

From inside the backpacks came a jumble of walking boots, cargo trousers, tracksuit bottoms, thick woollen socks, windbreakers, anoraks, fleeces, and boxer shorts.

All roomy men's sizes. There were three sleeping bags and six towels.

'One size fits all,' said Vandersteen.

Like three ladies off to find their inner selves on a hiking retreat, we ambled out of the woods in our windbreakers.

We decided to take a gamble on the first truckers' cafe we spotted along the main road that skirted the woods. The door slammed behind us, and a huddle of men around a large table set with standard-issue white crockery looked us up and down. They were all dressed differently, yet still managed to look like they were in uniform: caps, body warmers, baggy denims, and T-shirts with prints. There was no conversation to interrupt: they'd been staring at the TV and now they were staring at us. Anna gave them a nod and was rewarded with a swift poke in the ribs from Vandersteen. Behind the bar, a fat man stood polishing an elegantly curved beer glass. He arched an eyebrow. Through an open door at the far end of the room came the patter of water and the scent of shower gel.

Vandersteen gave a sniff and said, 'No smoking allowed these days?'

The fat man stopped polishing for a moment and replied, 'No.'

'Oh,' said Vandersteen.

One of the heads around the large table swivelled back to face the TV. The fat man placed the beer glass on a shelf, turned around, slung the tea towel over his shoulder, and sighed.

'Ladies,' he said, 'this is an establishment for truckers, not for hikers.'

'Yes,' said Vandersteen. 'So?'

'So don't slam the door on your way out,' said the fat man.

'And what makes you think we're not truckers?' said Vandersteen.

'What do you take me for?' he said. 'Your sweet old mother?'

'You've clearly never met my mother,' said Vandersteen, and glanced around the room ready to acknowledge a few titters from the audience. The audience was glued to the TV again.

The man leaned across the bar and lowered his voice. 'Remind me to tell you sometime just how sweet your mother is.'

He straightened up and scanned the room, too, primed to soak up his non-existent applause.

'So, if you wouldn't mind…' said the fat man.

Vandersteen blinked once and launched into one of her stories, a monologue about her old truck, complete with make, model, and all the places it had taken her. And by the way, she wondered, just how long had the man behind the bar been working there, 'cause this used to be Henk's boy Sjaak's place till it was taken over by Tasty Wilma who ended up with that fat bloke François, who insisted on serving up the kind of grub you get at French motorway service stations, complete with cheeseboard and a salad bar on wheels. The man behind the bar glared at Vandersteen as if she'd just whacked him one in the bollocks and then pulled a squirrel from her sleeve.

'We've still got the French menu,' he said. 'And as for that fat bloke François, you're looking at him.'

He pointed to a buffet display case. The salad bar on wheels was parked alongside.

'Oh,' said Vandersteen. 'I'd be lying if I said you hadn't changed much. How's it working out for you? The French menu?'

'Can't complain,' said François. 'Things are ticking over nicely. Wilma's up and left, though.'

The TV was showing a no-holds-barred re-enactment of the sinking of a ship from the 1930s, complete with thunderclaps, lightning bolts, and humungous black waves. A toothpick of a man emerged from the kitchen bearing a huge pan of scrambled eggs. The truckers at the table sat to attention, and the little man walloped their plates full. Meanwhile, Anna had sat down on a chair by the buffet and was staring intently at the screen. The ship's crew was clinging on to ropes for dear life. Off in the distance, a lifeboat capsized. Madness and mayhem was blasting from the tinny speakers on either side of the TV screen.

'What can you do?' I heard François say. 'They come and go, come and go. Such is life.'

'We're gasping for a coffee,' said Vandersteen. 'But I left my truck at home. And the weather's on the turn.'

The man shook his head pityingly, then shot a glance at Anna.

'Is she... uh... normal?' asked François.

'Accident,' said Vandersteen, and leaned across the bar. 'With her old man's tanker. A real horror story.'

'Well then, take a seat,' said François, and nodded to a table over in the far corner. 'And for God's sake get your kit out of sight. If word gets out I've had three woman backpackers in here, I'll spend the next ten years trying to live it down.'

'Any chance of a shower?' Vandersteen asked.

François reached under the counter and tossed her a key. 'Need any help scrubbing your back?'

We went over and sat at the small table in the corner, wedged between the one-armed bandit and the stairs that led down to the smell of shower gel. François brought our coffee over, black with a hint of grease.

'Friends of Wilma's,' he said sheepishly to a man at the large table who grabbed him by the sleeve. 'From way back.'

I took a sip of my coffee. Vandersteen headed downstairs for her shower.

We ate meatballs and slurped coffee. I thought about my mother. Sometimes, out of the blue, I find myself missing my mother's hands so intensely, the scent of her skin. We were what you'd call an average family, more or less, but one day I looked at her and thought: I really don't like you at all. I was there at her side when my father died. I was a good daughter, comforted her as best I could, and one day I decided never to visit her again. I just couldn't do it anymore.

I told Nelis, 'I'm not going back there again.'

'Right-oh,' he said.

The more you tell yourself you don't need somebody, the more you start to believe it. That's the worst thing of all. My mother probably believed it herself, and that's why she died alone.

'We can go to the island,' I told Anna and Vandersteen. 'I have a cottage there.'

After my parents died, the cottage became mine, but I never went back there. Nelis let his friends use it sometimes, but that had been years ago. I had no idea what state it was in.

'If we can find ourselves another car, we could get there in no time,' I said. 'The key's hidden in an old chest in the shed.'

'Now that's what I call a plan!' exclaimed Vandersteen, clapping her hands.

'Strictly speaking, the best place to lie low is a medium-sized town,' said Anna. 'In a country where the weather's not too cold. But an island sounds wonderful. It really does.'

'How do we get there?' asked Vandersteen. 'On the ferry? We'll never manage that without someone seeing us.'

'We can walk across the mudflats to the island. As a child I did it with my parents often enough. If you keep your wits about you, it only takes a couple of hours.'

I was in the mood to show off.

'If you want to disappear off the face of the Earth, you need to order takeaways instead of eating in restaurants,' said Anna. 'We're leaving behind all kinds of information about ourselves: fingerprints, DNA.'

'Did you pick that up from your brother?' asked Vandersteen. 'Your disappearing-off-the-face-of-the-Earth routine?'

Anna nodded.

'He's a mine of useful information,' said Vandersteen. 'Or did I just put my foot in it again?'

The truckers grunted and we looked up to see the TV screen fill with a portrait of Vandersteen. Blood pounded in my ears. I nudged Vandersteen and nodded at the TV. She swore under her breath. Mariska Kampschreur appeared. She was speaking to us directly, her low voice distorted by the speakers.

'So if you hear this message—Anna Vandersteen, Anna van Veen, and the Third Woman—please get in touch with me. I want nothing more than to speak to the three of you. Rest assured, I will personally guarantee your safety.'

Kampschreur flashed an inviting smile, and the phone number of the newsroom appeared at the bottom of the screen.

'We need to get out of here,' Vandersteen whispered.

No sooner had she spoken than a fat hand slammed the bill down on the table. Anna shifted in her seat. François loomed over us, blocking out light. In panic, Vandersteen fumbled around in her pocket for some banknotes.

'Downstairs exit, next to the toilets,' François hissed and pointed over his shoulder.

'We've got company,' he said. 'Forget the bill. Just get up slowly and make yourselves scarce.'

I peered cautiously around his fat arm. At the bar, a copper with a faraway look in his eyes was sipping coffee from a little white cup, one buttock perched on a barstool. His partner was outside, smoking a cigarette. One of the truckers from the large table had gone over to the bar and was waving his arms around wildly, spinning some yarn or other. It didn't seem to be making much of a dent in the copper's steely demeanour.

'Quick,' said François. 'With his repertoire, our Jan can hold someone's attention for all of sixty seconds.'

As inconspicuously as we could, we got up, squeezed our way past François, and headed downstairs. He followed us down, the keys on his belt jingling. We stopped for a moment at the frosted glass door and shouldered our backpacks.

'I've no idea whether what they're saying about you on TV is true, ladies. But if it's a choice between the pigs and three gals who appear out of nowhere and eat meatballs at my table…'

With a grunt, he opened the door for us. We made our way past an assembly of bins, rubbish bags, and empty oil drums. I looked back. François waved for a second and banged the door shut. We jumped over a ditch and ran for the cover of some nearby trees. Branches kept hitting me in the face, followed a split second later by a thump from my backpack, but the ordeal didn't last long as the trees thinned out into a meadow.

'What a country! You can never have a nice long woodland walk when you need one,' said Vandersteen. 'But woodland aside, I'm having one hell of a day.'

Anna and I looked at each other.

'Do you reckon they've launched a full-scale manhunt?' said Vandersteen. 'Looks to me like we're national news.'

'It's not something to cheer about,' said Anna.

'But it was *Mariska Kampschreur*!' beamed Vandersteen. 'She said my name. She knows I exist! She wants to meet me!'

'You didn't happen to take down her number?' I said. 'While we were getting ready to run for our lives?'

I whacked Vandersteen on her bony shoulder.

'We need to find out what's going on,' said Anna.

'But first,' I said, 'we need to stick to our plan and nick ourselves a car.'

Vandersteen picked up the pace.

'Point taken,' she said. 'Love can wait, ladies. But fate's wheels are in motion. You mark my words.'

We climbed over the umpteenth fence and marched along a shallow ditch in a direction we took to be north. According to Vandersteen, it was best to stick to the countryside, even more so on foot than by car. By the time they could pinpoint our whereabouts, we'd be in the woods a few miles further on, and by the time they'd mobilized enough manpower to comb the area, we'd be further on again in another patch of woodland. The most important thing was to avoid chance encounters with the boys in blue. And in that respect, too, the countryside was the best place to be, especially since the powers that be had closed down half the rural police stations.

A nickable car was nowhere to be found.

Darkness fell. We trudged along country roads, with only the occasional lamppost to light our way. Vandersteen claimed that even through the clouds she could navigate by the light of the moon and a few stars. I was tired. We'd been walking for hours and we could have been anywhere. There wasn't a soul to be seen. Suddenly, Anna stopped.

'We've been here before,' she said.

'What?' I said.

I looked around, worried we'd end up walking right back through the hospital doors if we didn't watch out.

'Where the hell are we?' I asked Vandersteen.

'That farmhouse, look!' Anna pointed.

We had come to a crossroads. Just across the way was a farm with barns and greenhouses.

'It looks exactly like the one we passed half an hour ago.'

'I thought it was weird that we hadn't hit a town or something by now,' said Vandersteen.

She put her arm round Anna's shoulder.

'We have two options,' I said. 'Either we find somewhere to bed down for the night, or we keep on walking.'

I put my hands on my hips and pretended to be thinking. Truth was, I just wanted to stand there for a minute—stand there and not move. Vandersteen hauled herself over a fence and set off toward the farmyard.

'Vandersteen,' I hissed. 'What do you think you're doing?'

She disappeared into a barn.

'Should we follow her?' said Anna.

Vandersteen stuck her head out the door and waved us over. I helped Anna over the fence, and we ploughed through the wet grass in our hiking boots.

Inside the barn we sat down on the ground in a corner behind some tractors. Electric drills and other tools were hanging on the wall.

'That's what I love about the countryside,' said Vandersteen. 'Here you can just leave the barn door open.' She took a drill down off the wall and started pressing the 'on' button. Each time the drill began to buzz, she jerked an arm or a leg or swung her torso from side to side in a wacky robot dance. Sometimes I wonder whether Vandersteen really existed, or whether I made her up. We laughed, Anna and I. We laughed till we cried and then we fell asleep.

'So.'

I looked up. A farmer was towering over us, leaning on a pitchfork. He looked exactly like you'd expect a farmer with a pitchfork to look.

'So,' he said again. 'Had a nice nap?'

I struggled out of my sleeping bag.

'Polish slaves?' asked the farmer. 'On the run? You from Poland?'

I shook my head. The other two were still sound asleep.

'Time to get up,' he said. 'Come into the house and I'll make you a sandwich.'

He turned and marched out of the barn. I shook the others awake.

We were on a roll: meatballs on the house at the truckers' cafe, and now we were about to tuck into a free sandwich. I wondered whether the farmer had a TV. He looked to me like the kind of man who always had a transistor radio yakking away in the background. I studied his face to see if he might have any inkling who we were. It looked like an old leather bag that had been lightly dusted with flour. His expression hadn't altered one iota since our first encounter back in the barn. Blank.

The kitchen door was half open and I could see a slice of living room: a pile of letters and documents on an oak dining table. No sign of a newspaper or a magazine. We munched our way through the farmer's bread and cheese and drank his coffee. He stood over by the kitchen sink with his arms crossed. No one said a word. When our plates were empty, he cleared them away and stacked them on the draining board. I downed the last of my coffee.

'I could drop you off somewhere in a bit,' said the farmer. 'At a petrol station or one of those spots where people pick up hitchhikers.'

'That's a good idea,' said Vandersteen.

'Hmm,' I said. 'I'm not sure that's such a good idea.'

'Where are we?' asked Anna. 'Do you know where we are?'

'No, the good man hasn't a clue where he lives,' said Vandersteen.

The farmer mentioned a place name. I looked at the others, but it was clear it meant nothing to any of us.

'Do you live here all on your own?' I asked.

Vandersteen kicked me under the table.

'Only asking,' I said.

I had to get a sense of what kind of man we were dealing with.

'Yup, all on my own,' said the farmer.

'Oh,' I said. 'It's a big operation for one man to run.'

'Aw, it's not so bad,' said the farmer. 'It's all automated. I have a milking robot.'

'Oh,' I said. 'That's nice.'

'Nice,' said the farmer. 'You could call it that.'

We fell silent again. The clock above the door ticked loudly.

'Doesn't it get lonely?' I asked. 'Out here all alone with your milking robot?'

'Anna… ' said Vandersteen in her sweetest voice.

'There's the cows,' said the farmer. 'And the seasonal workers. I've got greenhouses, too. Enough to keep me busy.'

'We're on the road,' said Vandersteen. 'But we got blown off course.'

'Yes,' said Anna. 'The coffee's great, by the way.'

The farmer topped up her cup again.

'Would you mind giving me a tour of the premises?' I said.

The farmer froze in mid-pour.

'A tour?'

'Yes,' I said.

'Of the farm?'

'Yes,' I said.

I took another kick in the shins.

'Come on, you two. It's not like I'm asking him to donate a kidney. I'm just curious,' I said.

'Perhaps the farmer has better things to do,' said Vandersteen.

The farmer cleared his throat.

'You can all have a tour.'

'I've never seen a milking robot,' I said.

The farmer straightened his glasses.

'Well, well,' he said. 'Who'd have thought? A tour guide on my own farm.'

I stood up. The farmer walked on ahead. Vandersteen

flashed me a ferocious stare. She was trying to signal to me, but I had no idea what she meant. I gave her a breezy thumbs up.

'Here we have the hall,' said the farmer. 'And upstairs are the bedrooms, but there's nothing much to see up there. This is a cupboard and there's the toilet. And the bathroom is here. Basic, but it fits the bill. We'll go outside in a sec, that's where it all happens. Indoors it's all a bit…'

'Basic,' I said. 'So this is the bathroom?'

Vandersteen heaved a sigh.

'Yes,' said the farmer.

He stood still for a moment.

'Mind if I take a peek?'

'Do you want a shower?'

'Oh, I'd love to see a real country shower.'

I was giving the farmer my best femme fatale. Behind his back, Vandersteen mimed banging her head against the wall. The farmer pulled open the bathroom door and with both hands I gave him an almighty shove. He sailed across the tiled floor.

'What the fu-u-uck…?' he shouted as he sailed.

I slammed the door shut and threw my whole weight against it.

'Get me a broom!' I yelled. 'Or a mop! Anything with a stick attached.'

The farmer began to hammer on the door. It was all I could do to keep him contained. 'Polish bitches!' he bawled.

In a panic, Vandersteen started yanking open every door in the hallway. I braced myself, but the farmer was strong. Vandersteen rushed up to me waving a plastic Christmas tree, branches all folded up. She rammed the tree between the door handle and the heating pipe next to the door. The farmer kept on pounding at the door and the Christmas tree proved to be surprisingly flexible.

'Find something broomsticky!' Vandersteen yelled at Anna, while we both strained to hold the door shut. Anna ran back into the kitchen.

'Sorry, mister,' I shouted. 'Don't take it personally!'

He roared at us to open the door. Anna had managed to lay her hands on his pitchfork. I slid it into place alongside the Christmas tree. The pounding continued, but the door didn't budge. I sank to the floor. Anna patted my head. Meanwhile, Vandersteen raided the key cabinet on the wall.

'Good,' I said. 'Give me a moment.'

I counted to ten and got up. Nothing else for it but to follow through with our plan, or what passed for one. We filed out of the farmhouse.

'Wine!' I exclaimed. 'I don't care where, I don't care when, but today I want a glass of wine. I'll swig it straight from the bottle if I have to.'

I marched across the yard to the farmer's other barn. The door creaked open to reveal a beautiful old rust-brown Mercedes-Benz. Vandersteen started casing the joint. At the back of the barn were two sliding doors that led to the greenhouses behind. She stuck her nose in the air.

'Hang on,' she said.

'What?' I said.

Vandersteen followed her nose all the way back to the

sliding doors. She took one more sniff and rolled the doors aside.

On the island, there were days when I could hear the carousel on the village square. 'The wind's blowing in the right direction,' my father would say. 'Sound travels on the wind. Just like scent. If you want to sneak up on a deer, you have to stand downwind of him, otherwise he'll smell you coming.'

He stuck a finger in his mouth and thrust it in the air.

'Look,' he said. 'Wet your finger and you can feel where the wind is coming from.'

I turned my face to the wind and closed my eyes.

'I can feel it fine like this,' I said.

My father lowered his finger.

'So you can,' he said.

He closed his eyes, too. And there we stood.

'Come on, Vandersteen,' said Anna. 'We need to get out of here.'

'Check the keys you took,' I called over my shoulder. 'Maybe we can nick the Merc.'

'Ooooh!' exclaimed Anna. 'Tomatoes!'

Vandersteen let out a sudden whoop of delight from somewhere in the middle of the greenhouse.

'Anna!' yelled Anna.

I squeezed past the Mercedes and ran into the greenhouse. They were both lost among the tomatoes somewhere, but I could see the twine attached to the tomato stakes twitching. I dived in among the plants and made a beeline for their voices. Now I could smell it, too, a strange aroma. Through the prickly, summery scent of the tomatoes there was a distinct smell of something else. It grew stronger and more pungent the closer I came, and right before I pushed aside the last tomato plant, it dawned on me.

'Weed,' I said.

'That's my girl,' said Vandersteen.

Anna stood there gawping. Vandersteen took hold of the tip of a cannabis plant and sniffed her fingertips.

'Sticky,' she said. 'Good shit.'

She tugged at the top of the plant with all her might. It trembled as if determined to shake off this scrawny little woman who was wrestling it to the ground.

'Flippin' 'eck!' said Vandersteen.

She pulled her tobacco pouch from her back pocket, and with the nails of one hand she crumbled some of the top of the plant into a cigarette paper.

'Okay, so it's not wine,' she said. 'But sometimes you've got to take your pleasures where you find them. Am I right?'

'I think we should get going,' I said.

'Are you honestly going to sit there and smoke a joint?' said Anna. 'I don't believe it!'

'We'll be out of here soon enough,' said Vandersteen. 'But first... a little light relaxation.'

She lit the joint, took a couple of decent puffs, and held it out to me.

'Well, Annie,' she said. 'Fancy a toke?'

An hour later I was flat on my back among the tomato plants.

'You know what it is?' I said. 'You know what it is? Why I said nothing about that man of mine? That man of mine was a complete and utter bastard. He was having it off with any old tart. After twelve years of marriage, I came home and found him at it one night. Stood there and watched that big white backside of his bouncing up and down. Jesus, I thought. Je-sus Chrrrist. And you know what the crazy thing is? Well? Well? Well?'

I paused for effect.

'So now you're playing finish-the-sentence?' said Vandersteen.

'I was almost glad. Right there, right then, I thought, here's my cue. Exit stage left. At long last I can just pack up my things and leave.'

I gazed up at the roof of the greenhouse. Birds, clouds—it's one big moving work of art, I thought. A moving photo exhibition.

'Life's a moving photo exhibition,' I said. 'With cracks in the glass, hinges, and iron frames. Rusty iron frames. Pointy glass roofs repeating over and over.'

Pleased with myself, I took another drag on the joint that Anna handed to me. She was lying beside me on the path, her head on Vandersteen's lap.

'Do you get what I mean?'

'Totally,' said Anna.

'But did I do it? Did I pack my things? Did I hell! That would've been way too easy. No, I hung around for weeks, without saying a word.'

A bird slammed into the glass roof of the greenhouse at full speed.

I jumped.

'Bloody hell!' said Vandersteen.

The bird lay still on the roof for a moment. A hawfinch, I guessed. Not many of them around, anymore. Then it slid slowly down the glass. It would have been a lovely little bird to stuff and mount. A hawfinch. I've never held one in my hands.

'Oh, never mind,' I said.

'I'm hungry,' said Anna. She sat up and picked a tomato.

'I resorted to a bomb scare to get Angelique back,' said Vandersteen. 'A bomb scare at the station.'

Tomato juice dribbled down Anna's chin.

'And?' I said. 'Did it work?'

'No,' said Vandersteen.

'Hey,' said Anna, 'was that last winter, by any chance?'

'That's the one!' exclaimed Vandersteen, perking up.

'I was there!' shouted Anna.

'Never! Really?' shouted Vandersteen. 'Wow! That's amazing!'

'I remember seeing it on the news,' I said. 'Was that you?'

'Angelique was taking the train to her mother's. Kids in tow. I told you that already, didn't I? I was supposed to pack up and leave. Off to your mother's then, are you? I thought. We'll see about that.'

'That's when I met Leendert!' cried Anna.

'No! You're kidding!' said Vandersteen.

'It was ten below zero and no one could get home. People were fighting for a place on the bus. No one was allowed within fifty feet of the station, so I ended up going into a fast-food place for a coffee. It'll all blow over in a while, I thought. I mean, I've never heard of people not getting home.'

'I once heard about this woman in India,' I said. 'Well, she was a girl at the time. Got on the wrong bus one day. Fifty years later she got home. Fifty years later!'

'Yes, but that's India for you,' said Anna. 'Behind the times, they are.'

'You can talk,' said Vandersteen. 'With your brother and his jerrycan.'

Anna gave a little sigh. I handed her back the joint.

'Anyway, as I was saying, there I was, standing at one of those shelf thingies that run the length of the window, watching the crowds go by, and all of a sudden he came over and stood next to me. With a cup of coffee in his hand. A real looker. Normally I wouldn't know what to say, but in a weird situation like that it's much easier to strike up a conversation. Two hours later, we were still standing there. Eventually we took a taxi home. And that's where we had our first kiss.'

Anna gave a little squeal.

'Oh, honestly. It's not like me at all! But it was so cold and I was so tired and I thought: I'm just going to do it. I thought my heart was going to explode!'

'How about that,' beamed Vandersteen, waving her hand in Anna's direction. Anna passed her the joint. 'It's so gratifying to think something good came of that bomb scare.'

My thoughts wandered back to the news that day. Nelis had got home late, too. He'd managed to squeeze onto a bus, he said. Without having to resort to violence. The entire station had been sealed off until midnight. The weather was freezing and hundreds of people had ended up spending the night in a school gym. Suddenly it dawned on me. I jolted upright.

'But didn't they make an arrest?' I said. 'They got the person who did it! Was that you?'

'Yes, Sherlock, that was me.'

'And they put you behind bars.'

'And not for the first time,' said Vandersteen.

'Yeah, that penny dropped a while back,' I said.

'When you start out on the path of deceit... ' said Vandersteen. She relit what was left of the joint and inhaled deeply.

'Uh... well... uh, you keep on going down the path of deceit,' she said, puffing smoke. 'And sometimes it's a narrow path, and one helluva long path, too.'

She flicked the stub in among the tomatoes.

'All done.'

Anna sat up.

'Listen, you two, we need to get moving.'

'Yes,' I said. 'This is insane.'

We stood up, giggling away to ourselves.

'But it's almost fun,' said Anna. 'Better than hospital. Or home, for that matter.'

We nodded.

'Shouldn't we go and check on the farmer?' Anna asked.

Vandersteen started stuffing her pockets full of weed. Anna dusted down her clothes. I wove my way through the tomato plants back to the barn. Everything was just as we'd left it. There wasn't a breath of wind. It was like walking into a photograph. I fished a handful of keys from Vandersteen's backpack and approached the old Merc. Today, everything seemed to be going our way.

Vandersteen slid behind the steering wheel.

'We'll take turns,' she said. 'You can drive, can't you?'

'Not very well,' I said.

I'm that woman doing fifty on the motorway. Nelis and I always wound up having a blazing row whenever I took the wheel. One day I refused to do it anymore. Hey presto, no more rows. Sometimes people make life way too complicated. The old Merc eased out of the barn. I found a tatty road map in the pocket of the door.

'Look,' I said.

Vandersteen turned onto our oh-so-familiar cross-roads and took off down a country road. She snatched the map from my lap and gave it a once-over.

'This thing's so old, it doesn't even have Flevoland on the front,' she said.

'These country roads were around way before the powers that be felt the need to reclaim a whole new province from the sea,' I said, snatching back the map. 'When did they build Flevoland, anyway?'

'I said Flevoland, not Legoland,' sighed Vandersteen. 'They didn't *build* it.'

'Well when did they... ' I said. 'What *do* you call that?'

'Don't ask me,' said Vandersteen. 'Maybe they sprayed it on.'

'Whereabouts were we again?' I said.

'Somewhere beginning with howthefuckshouldIknow,' said Vandersteen.

'We should drive into a village,' I said. 'At least then we'll know where we are.'

I flicked through the map.

'That poor man has no one,' Anna said. 'We shouldn't

have left him there like that. He gave us breakfast. He was going to help us.'

'Um… lest we forget,' I said, 'he's the proud owner of a marijuana plantation. Somehow, I don't think calling the police will be his first move, once he's rammed his way out of his bathroom.'

'A farmer goes mad if you lock him up,' said Anna.

'Yes,' said Vandersteen. 'It's a known fact.'

'Tomorrow or the day after, the man with the milk truck will turn up and take a look around. Our big, strapping farmer will last one day without food. And he's got his milking robot to keep things ticking over.'

Anna went quiet. We had a full tank of petrol, and on a full tank there was every chance we'd make it to the coast. The radio was churning out football results and spinning golden oldies. The car hummed along like an old sewing machine. I looked down at the map and traced a line across it.

'In a way, it's handy the map's so old,' I said. 'We're steering clear of the motorways, after all.'

'I need a wee,' said Anna.

Vandersteen adjusted the mirror.

'My last car was a bright-green Opel Kadett Coupé,' said Vandersteen. 'An old banger if ever there was one, but the best car I ever had. Thump the door on the driver's side and the window would slide all the way down. You could wind it back up again. Handy in summer. I got the door open with a kirby grip one time when I was drunk and I'd lost my keys. The fuel gauge didn't work either, but that was okay 'cause I always had a jerrycan of petrol in the boot. If she started to slow down all of a sudden

I'd pull over, pour in the jerrycan, and head for the nearest petrol station. If I'm honest, it made life more fun. One day you wake up with everything, and you miss the bad old days when everything you owned was falling to bits.'

The green of the trees shot past above us. It was lovely here, lovely and green. There's nothing quite like the green of leaves washed by the rain. We chugged along the country roads doing around fifty. Vandersteen turned up the radio. We were on again.

The presenter revealed that the car stolen at the hospital had now been recovered, and that the manhunt had been stepped up. Mariska Kampschreur was the special guest in the studio. Her sultry voice vibrated through the crackling speakers. She said our getaway had captured the public imagination and her team had received a record number of reports and inquiries about the three women on the run. She understood the appeal: we were a modern-day Bonnie & Clyde, only more like Bonnie & Bonnie & Bonnie. Three smart women who, for their own baffling reasons, had resorted to violence to evade the authorities and the long arm of the law. Mariska admitted that we had captured *her* imagination, too. As she saw it, Vandersteen was the driving force behind our little gang, the mastermind. No one knew what we were up to, but the Third Woman, as Anna has come to be called, surely held the key to the mystery.

'There's more at stake here than three criminals running from the law,' said Mariska. 'The authorities are afraid to lose face, and have launched what amounts to a witch-hunt. There are things we do not know. Things that no one knows. No one except these three women.'

'My, she's a smart cookie,' said Vandersteen.

The Third Woman was the enigma at the heart of this story. Where had this mentally disabled young woman come from?

'I'm not mentally disabled!' Anna yelled.

Back in the studio, someone else had pulled up a chair, and the conversation turned to the rest of the day's news. Vandersteen lowered the volume.

'Do you still need a wee?' Vandersteen asked Anna. 'We can pull over now. I'll join you. Annie? Peeing in the wild is one of life's undiluted pleasures.'

We were driving up a gentle incline, past an idyllic little lake. No sooner had the old Merc popped its nose over the crest of the hill than Vandersteen turned off the engine.

'This'll do nicely,' she said.

We got out of the car. Trees as far as the eye could see. I put my arms around Anna and Vandersteen's shoulders. The day was at its peak as we strolled down the hillside.

By the time I'd pulled up my trousers, Vandersteen was already lighting another joint.

'We should lay off the wacky baccy till we reach the island,' I said.

'Oh no you don't,' said Vandersteen. 'For weeks, I've been climbing the walls without a fag end to my name, and now our pockets are full.'

'We've no time to lose,' I said.

Vandersteen offered me the joint, and I caved in.

'Oh well,' I said. 'I suppose it is a holiday of sorts.'

'Yes,' said Anna. 'Run-for-your-life holidays.'

'Complete with dream kitchen,' said Vandersteen.

'And hot tub,' said Anna.

I took another couple of drags. In the distance I could hear the motorway. No matter where you are in this country, there's always a motorway within earshot, if the wind's blowing in the right direction. Except on the island, that is. Anna sat down on a tree trunk and sank her teeth into another tomato.

'We should move the car,' I said. 'It's perched up there like a flag on a mountain top. I'll park her in among the bushes. I mean, how many pedestrians am I going to mow down out here in the middle of nowhere?'

Vandersteen tossed me the keys. Chuckling, I headed up to the car. It was warm inside. I slid the key into the ignition. If my aim was half decent, I could steer the Merc in among those elderberry bushes. I turned the key.

'Hill start!' I shouted out of the window. 'The only thing I was ever any good at.'

Vandersteen gave me a thumbs up.

I stepped on the accelerator and eased up on the clutch till the car growled and dipped. With a theatrical flourish, I released the handbrake. The car shot backward. In blind panic, I jammed my foot harder on the accelerator, and the old Merc hurtled down the slope in reverse and plunged into the water.

Hands on hips we stood and stared at the car, half-submerged in our idyllic little lake. We had nearly busted a gut trying to tow it out, but all to no avail.

'Those backpacks will have had a good old soaking by now.'

Vandersteen was holding the dripping road map between thumb and forefinger.

'Yes,' I said.

'I can't say fate's been smiling on us. Transport-wise,' said Vandersteen.

'It's God's punishment,' said Anna. 'I know it is.'

'If this is the worst He can do after all the punishment you've had so far, I'd say He's losing His touch.'

Every now and then, bubbles gurgled up from the place where the boot must be.

'Will you rescue the bags?' said Vandersteen.

I stared at the bubbles. It was all I could do to soften the blow of losing the car.

'I'll say one thing for the Big Man: he has a sense of humour,' Vandersteen said to Anna.

Vandersteen began to chuckle, and Anna tried to suppress a giggle but failed.

'Come on, you two,' I said. 'Please. This isn't the time or the place.'

'Sorry,' said Anna, laughing even louder.

Vandersteen creased up with her hands on her knees and began to roar.

'Sorry,' said Anna again. 'I can't help it. Honest, I can't.'

Tears were streaming down her cheeks. I kicked off my soaking boots, peeled off my wet trousers, followed by my underwear and my sweaters, and waded back into the water. Vandersteen looked up, saw me struggling through the water in nothing but my bra, and slapped

Anna's shoulder with the back of her hand. Anna wiped the tears from her eyes.

'Okay, okay!' I shouted. 'I get the message.'

Vandersteen spluttered something about 'wet bra, no panties' and 'God bless her and all who sail in her.' I decided to concentrate on the car. When I got around the back, I reached underwater and yanked the boot open. A huge pocket of air burst out, and a surge of water splattered my face. I hauled the three sodden backpacks out of the boot. By this stage, Anna had crumpled into a heap on the grass. From where I was standing, their gales of laughter sounded like an old broadcast of *Sunday Night at the Palladium*, where there was always some woman laughing louder than everyone else, her hysterical 'woo-hoo-hoo' setting the whole audience off again. Weighed down by the backpacks, I battled my way to the water's edge.

'Tits ahoy!' yelled Vandersteen.

Anna rocked with laughter till she collapsed onto her back.

'That's it!' I growled, once I'd lugged all three backpacks onto dry land. 'We're dumping the weed. Now! We'll never get anywhere staggering cross-country like three old stoners.'

While I got dressed, Vandersteen emptied her pockets into the water. She put her arm around me. 'A nice juicy red herring for when they trace the car back to Old MacDonald and his farm.'

'So, now what?' said Anna.

'Now?' said Vandersteen. 'Now we walk.'

I squelched along behind the others in my wet boots.

I was sitting in my old easy chair nursing a bottle of beer, Hetty on the sideboard next to me. The sliding doors were open, and I sat and watched Nelis's guests out on the deck of the houseboat, drinking and laughing. I didn't know anyone. I wondered if she was at the party. The more I think back on that evening, the more it blends in with everything else in my life. There I sat, a rank amateur, flailing desperately inside. I sipped my beer and watched Nelis slapping records onto the turntable; I watched as his friends danced. On the stretch of deck we used as a balcony, sausages were sizzling on a gas-fired barbecue. I didn't say much. I'm not sure anyone noticed. I kept myself to myself and smiled up at Nelis when he came and stood next to me. When he asked for a kiss, I kissed him. As long as the outside world believes it, the pretence is easier to maintain: nothing's wrong, everything's hunky-dory. The best stopgap there is. I watched as the sausages were lifted onto a plate, one by one.

We came to a fence around a children's farm at the edge of a playground.

'Playgrounds at night are even creepier than graveyards,' said Vandersteen.

The swings swayed slowly to and fro in the wind. Every now and then I heard the sound of something cracking. A house stood at the edge of the woods, all its windows dark. Vandersteen peered through the wire mesh and pointed.

'There we have it,' she said. 'Supper on a stick.'

'Okay,' said Anna.

She walked over to the side of the road, leaned against a tree and gave us the all clear.

Vandersteen clawed her way up the fence and elegantly swung her leg over the top. I followed as best I could. She opened the little door to the chicken run and popped her head in. Nothing stirred. She leaned in a little further, and a furious cackling erupted. She pulled a chicken out of the hatch, feet first. Sand, dust, and droppings flew out from beneath its flapping wings.

'Chicken shit,' said Vandersteen, hiding her nose in the sleeve of her coat. 'Right, now it's your turn.'

I thought of Hetty. Back at the fence, Vandersteen handed me her catch. There I stood like Jesus on the cross with a chicken thrashing away in either hand.

'What now?' I shouted, once Vandersteen had landed on the other side of the fence.

I had to close my eyes with all the dust the chickens were whipping up around me.

'Throw.'

'What?' I said.

I'd heard her all right.

'How's it going?' Anna shouted from the roadside.

'Throw?' I said.

'Got a better plan?' said Vandersteen.

Anna came over to join us.

'Go on, throw,' said Vandersteen. 'We'll catch them.'

'Let me look for a gate!' I shouted.

'There is no gate!'

'Throw!' Anna shouted.

Anna and Vandersteen stepped away from each other,

arms outstretched like a couple of goalies in the middle of a penalty shoot-out.

'The world's gone mad,' I muttered.

I bent my knees, swung my arms like a Russian ballet dancer, and hurled the chickens over the fence with all my might.

'For Chrissake! Not both at once!' Vandersteen wailed.

Anna and Vandersteen scurried after the scared-to-death chickens. I scrambled up the fence, lost my balance at the top, and came crashing down on other side. I'm too old for this, I thought, as I lay there gazing up at the clouds that sailed over. They can all come and get me, I thought. The police. Anna's brother. They can chuck me in the deepest, darkest dungeon, I don't care. Just let me lie here.

Vandersteen's face popped into view. She was clutching a chicken in either hand. Anna's face followed.

'Ready to go?' Anna asked.

I nodded, and jumped to my feet.

'Ready as I'll ever be.'

'So where did you learn to bone a chicken like that?' asked Vandersteen.

The two chickens from the children's farm were roasting over a campfire. They smelled like heaven.

'You know your way around a knife.'

'I started young,' I said.

It's not that difficult, once you get the knack. For me, the tricky thing about taxidermy is making the form, not to mention finding the right pose, and making sure the skin fits snugly. Not too tight and not too loose.

'Can you do that with other animals, too?'

I can prepare anything. I did a calf once. There was even a llama.

'Mainly birds,' I said. 'But the principle's the same.'

'What about pigs?' Vandersteen asked. 'Ever polished off a porker?'

'Pigs?' I said.

'I'm talking dinner, here,' said Vandersteen. 'You never know what we might come across. What else would you do with them?'

'I like to stuff birds. At home I had a room full of beautiful birds, all stuffed and mounted.'

There. I'd said it.

'Oh,' said Vandersteen. 'That's nice.'

'It's just a hobby,' I said.

Anna looked at me long and hard.

'Interesting,' said Vandersteen.

'There you have it,' I said. 'I do everything but pluck them.'

My birds went up in flames. They burn easily if you make the form of gauze and jute, which is what I prefer to do, even with the small animals. I only use Styrofoam now and again. For me, it's too dry, too light. What was left of the boat was dismantled at the shipyard. The berth is for sale. I'd be able to live off the proceeds for a while… if I could get at the money… if our pursuers never caught up with us… if we ever made it to the island. Suddenly it all seemed so far away. And supposing we did make it to the island, who was to say we'd be safe? My heart sank, my courage fled. I thought of the miles of woodland we still had to plough through, the rivers of rain that would fall on us. How long could we keep up the absurd pretence that we were three lady hikers sponsored by the knitting bee of the local old-folk's association? The news had described Anna as 'burned from head to toe.' No one who saw us would need a mugshot to put two and two together. One phone call to the police, and that would be the end. A manhunt was underway, and here we were blundering around, taking one risk after another. Were they already hot on our heels? I sighed and half-hoped they would catch us. At least that would put an end to the anxiety, imagining a man in a windbreaker with a dog and a mobile phone lurking behind every tree. Yet, anxious or not, we had a plan, and no choice but to stick to it.

'We have to get to the island as fast as we can,' I said. 'Once we're safe, we can take it from there.'

'It takes between seven and ten years for your identity to disappear from all the databases,' said Anna. 'And if one of us gets a job, it'll have to be working night shift. That way, you limit your contact with other people.'

'I'll go back to work,' said Vandersteen.

I shook my head.

'It's about time you took early retirement,' I said.

'I'll be the judge of that,' said Vandersteen.

'And you have to change jobs regularly. That's a tall order on an island.'

'We'll lie low for a while, and then one of us will make a go of it, whoever's had the least exposure. Once the hype has died down, people will start to forget our faces.'

'Shaving your hair off like that was a smart move, after all,' said Anna.

'I'll eat myself silly and put on a few pounds,' said Vandersteen. 'No problem.'

'Where the hell are you going to find enough food to put on a few pounds?' I said.

'I can work wonders with a squirrel,' said Vandersteen. 'Squirrel casserole. Tastes like rabbit. Of course, you have to pick all the ticks out of the pelt, and there's not much meat on their bones. Catching them's a dying art. You should see me shin up a tree. With an animal like that, it's all about the element of surprise.'

Vandersteen leaned back contentedly and lit up a ciggie.

'Any more questions, Van Veen?'

I shook my head.

'Tomorrow the hike continues.'

When the flames had all but died away, we crawled into our sleeping bags.

'Oh, I do love the countryside,' said Vandersteen, after we'd nicked a newspaper from a mailbox. 'It cuts me to the quick, to the quick I tell you, that we have no choice but to abuse the simple virtues that make me love the countryside so much. Not a locked door in sight, not even a barn door, not even if you have a marijuana plantation out back. And a mailbox so far from your front door, you have to hop on the bike to pick up your post. That's the life!'

Anna had an air of serenity about her as she walked along with the freshly printed paper tucked under her arm. The front page featured photos of Vandersteen and me, and a black silhouette of a third head with a question mark stamped on it. A banner headline promised reams of juicy revelations about our exploits. We were almost out of rations, so we decided to make the most of what we had and brew some coffee, fry up some bacon, and sit down with the morning paper. A roadside map told us there was a lake up ahead where we could have a dip, wash our clothes, and get a fire going.

'We'll sit down like decent folk,' said Vandersteen. 'Complete with our morning paper.'

We were all really looking forward to it. You have to make your own fun in life, whatever the circumstances. Anna even had a little bounce in her step.

The newspaper lay at my feet, neatly folded. An immaculate morning paper. Down at the lake, I could hear Anna and Vandersteen squealing in the cold water. I opened the paper carefully. Page two was almost entirely devoted to us. They still didn't know who Anna was, and an appeal was made to readers to phone in any tips they had. Meanwhile, Mariska Kampschreur was pursuing her own line of inquiry. Her offer to meet us was still on the table, complete with phone number. That would perk Vandersteen up no end. We'd soon be national celebrities, at this rate. I was about to get up, stroll down to the water's edge, and read out the news to Anna and Vandersteen. I turned the page to see how much more the paper had to say about us, and I froze.

There it was. In inky black capitals.

Happy people. Happy pigs emblazoned on the side of a truck. The music had lured everyone inside, and

I stepped out onto the deck. I could see them dancing through the living-room windows. The barbecue was cooling down, people had bread rolls in their hands, bottles of beer. I went over and stood by the barbecue and stared out across the water, taking in the ripples on the surface, the distant contours of the docked freighters. I looked down at the gas canister, and I thought. I thought for a long time. I told the policemen who questioned me at the hospital that I had acted on impulse, but it was no impulse. I had been thinking about it for weeks. It had started out as a fantasy, wormed its way into my head on nights when I couldn't sleep. I thought about how I'd go about it, just like my daydreams at primary school: every day I'd dream a little more, every day I'd add a detail or two. I had imagined every aspect of how it would feel—my revenge. Nelis was surprised when I suggested buying a gas-fired barbecue. I'd never been one for new-fangled contraptions. 'It's not a barbecue without charcoal,' I always used to say. He thought I was doing him a favour. I had carried the grey gas canister out onto the deck myself that morning. Here it was, and here I was. In the background, the ripples continued to play across the water. I fished a lighter from my pocket and fiddled with the tube on the canister till it came loose with a short hiss. Inside, the party people danced on. I turned the valve, and the smell of gas slowly curled its way into my nostrils. Turning my back on the water, I flicked the lighter and held it at arm's length. Like a crème brûlée torch in overdrive, a flame spurted from the mouth of the canister and burned a hole in my jeans. The pain that shot through my leg barely registered. I looked down at the scorched denim in surprise. It hadn't been part of the plan. Then I turned my attention back to the flame, still burning strong. I saw a few people inside look my way and nudge one another. Someone knocked on the window. I grabbed the flaming canister, took a couple of paces toward the sliding doors and, with everything I had in me, I hurled it through the glass. I saw Nelis jump to his feet. I recall every detail. The look on his face. I once heard a serial killer say he believed that every person he'd let pass through his life without being murdered was a life he'd saved. He had a point. I never thought I'd be able to do such a thing. And no, I'm not crazy. This was no psychotic episode. It was like standing on a balcony way up high and being afraid you might step off into space. That was it exactly: I was afraid I'd do it, and then I did it anyway. Some people say they feel the urge to destroy something beautiful out of frustration; with me it was the urge, the uncontrollable urge, to destroy something that was pretending to be beautiful. I took a few steps back. Inside, bottles of alcohol fell to the floor. The carpet caught fire in an instant. People screamed, people fell, flames raced up the curtains, gnawed through the boat's wooden walls, and there, at the centre of it all, was my husband's face. Then came the explosion—a bright flash, a thunderclap, and a force that threw me off the deck. Glass splintered and flew in all directions. Flames licked at my skin and my clothes caught fire. All I could see was fire and my arms thrust out in front of me, clawing at flames that seemed to be shooting out of my sleeves. I hit the water, went under, and then there was nothing.

He had showed me the spot when we were out walking one day. I have no way of knowing if it's where he's been laid to rest.

'That's the place, Annie,' he said that day. 'That's where we'll lie, side by side under that big oak tree.'

I don't know whether he ever told anyone else, mentioned it to any of his friends. Perhaps, toward the end, he had dreamed of lying next to her under the big oak tree.

'A place like that would cost the Earth,' I said.

'Ah,' he said. 'But by then, money won't matter anymore.'

'Yeah... no... exactly,' I said.

The place where the houseboat was is empty now, in any case.

I don't know the names of the people who died, or whether she was among them. Nelis is the only name I know for sure. My lawyer told me when he came to see me at the hospital, when I still had a room to myself. After the fact, there were enough people who were able to testify that it was all my doing. Nelis didn't know that I knew what I knew. That's something I carry with me.

And there it all was in black and white, alongside a photo of me with Nelis, and a photocopy of the bill for the gas canister in my name. There were two eyewitness accounts by friends of Nelis's who will go through life disfigured, thanks to me. They said I had refused to talk, that I had shown no remorse, that I had got off lightly by diving into the water while they had been trapped in a floating inferno. I hardly recognized any of the names.

I scrunched the pages into a ball and stared into space. Anna and Vandersteen were still splashing around and laughing.

By the time they came out of the water, shivering, I had a small fire going. The coffee pot was bubbling away among the flames and giving off a fine aroma.

'A campfire, that's the spirit,' said Vandersteen, once she'd got dressed. 'I didn't know you had it in you.'

'Home is where the hearth is.'

'How did you manage that?'

'Oh, you know. Gathered some sticks together and then lit them with a bit of the paper.'

'A bit of the newspaper?' said Anna.

Vandersteen picked up the remaining pages.

'Don't tell me you tossed that article about us onto the fire… ' said Vandersteen, snapping the newspaper shut and throwing it aside indignantly.

I looked her straight in the eye.

'No, did I really?' I said.

Something popped among the flames. Vandersteen held my gaze.

'Imagine you not noticing a little thing like that,' she said.

'Oh dear,' I replied.

Vandersteen cocked an eyebrow.

'And I suppose you didn't think to read what they'd written about us?'

'No,' I said.

'For fuck's sake,' said Vandersteen.

'Uh… ' I said.

'Why on Earth did you… ?'

I shrugged my shoulders.

'Dunno,' I said.

I shifted my gaze to Anna, who looked at Vandersteen, then at me, then back at Vandersteen. Vandersteen bent down and poked the fire with a stick.

'Did you really throw our article onto the fire?' said Anna, disappointed. 'I was so looking forward to reading it.'

'It was an accident,' I said. 'I was trying so hard to get the wood to catch fire.'

Anna scanned the rest of the pages. Vandersteen fished a charred section of newspaper from among the flames.

'Well, what have we here?' she said, and shot me a dirty look. 'Maybe we can piece a thing or two together, after all.'

I could have played the crying game. Maybe I should have played the crying game. Maybe that would've been the smart thing to do. But the crying game only works if you can cry real tears.

'I hope so,' I shrugged. 'Sorry.'

Vandersteen picked apart the charred and tattered scraps of paper.

'Ripley's ornamental fireplaces,' she read aloud.

'Sorry,' I said again.

Vandersteen thrust a hiking boot into the flames, stamped twice, and the fire was out. Then she began to stuff her newly washed clothes into her backpack.

'Let's go,' she said. 'You'll have to get washed another time. And keep your mitts off the next newspaper.'

Anna still didn't seem to twig what had happened. We

shouldered our packs and began to walk again, leaving the newspaper behind in the grass.

With a crack of thunder as an overture, it began to rain.

'That dreadful summer of ours is over at last,' I said chirpily, in the hope of lightening the mood.

'I hate it when people say that kind of thing,' said Anna. 'I really do. One drop of rain, and summer's over. It's September! Of course summer's over. Why should I care about your stupid summer?'

Vandersteen looked at me and shook her head. I squeezed Anna's shoulder. We walked on, rain tapping on the hood of my old anorak. My two-sizes-too-big hiking boots had lost the will to keep out water since the incident with the Merc, but my feet were still warm thanks to my three pairs of wet socks. We came to a halt at one of those little toadstool markers that shows walkers the way. Vandersteen clicked on the torch and squinted at the road map. Anna's arms hung heavy at her sides. Water ran from her hood and trickled in front of her eyes like one of those kitschy fountains next to the till at a Chinese restaurant. I peered over Vandersteen's shoulder. She pointed at a dot on the map and then at the toadstool. We looked back at the map. Vandersteen flipped it and pointed at another spot. I nodded and mumbled in agreement. The Chinese fountain hadn't moved a muscle, just heaved a sigh when Vandersteen flipped the map again.

'Or... uh... or ... ' said Vandersteen, tracing another line with her finger.

The edges of the map were bloated with rain.

'Hmmmm,' I said, and nodded.

It rained.

'Yes, or… ' I said, flipping the map again.

And rained.

'Look.'

And rained.

'I see,' said Vandersteen. 'Yeah… could do… could do.'

Anna sat down in a puddle. She crossed her arms.

'So?' she asked.

'We keep walking, of course,' said Vandersteen.

Anna heaved another sigh.

'It would help if you stopped your moaning for a while,' I said.

'I didn't say a word,' said Anna.

'That sighing of yours is getting on my nerves.'

'But I'm not moaning.'

'You are moaning.'

'I can do whatever I like.'

'Uh,' I said, 'that's not strictly true.'

'And why can't I do whatever I like?'

'Do I really have to spell it out for you?'

'I'm in pain,' said Anna.

'Walk,' said Vandersteen. She glanced at the map, stuck her nose in the air, and set off. I followed.

'You two treat me like a child,' said Anna.

'Well, stop acting like one,' I shouted over my shoulder.

'I'm not acting like a child!' she shouted.

'Then get a bloody move on,' said Vandersteen.

'But I don't feel well,' said Anna.

'What's the matter?' said Vandersteen.

'Stop exaggerating,' I said.

'Everything hurts,' said Anna.

'Where does it hurt?' said Vandersteen.

'Everywhere,' said Anna.

'All right, then,' Vandersteen relented.

'Seriously?' I said. 'You're going to fall for that?'

'Shut up for a minute,' said Vandersteen. 'What do you want to do, love?'

'I don't want to have to walk anymore.'

'I understand,' said Vandersteen. 'We all feel the same way.'

I fished the tobacco pouch from Vandersteen's back pocket and began to roll myself a cigarette. I lit it in the rain. First time. Everything was just peachy. Vandersteen had sat down on the ground next to Anna.

'I want to stay here,' said Anna.

'I understand,' said Vandersteen. 'I understand, but now's not the time. We have to keep moving. In a while, we'll sit ourselves down and take it easy. Read a book. Steal a chicken… How does that sound?'

'Read a book, steal a chicken,' I echoed Vandersteen in a silly voice.

'And after that?' Anna asked.

'If we can find ourselves a decent place to shelter, then we'll stay there and rest for the day.'

'You can't be serious?' I said.

'I don't see why not,' said Vandersteen. 'It's Tuesday. People are out at work.'

'Well, I say we should leave her here and press on,' I said to Vandersteen.

'Uh… you were the one who founded this little club of ours,' said Vandersteen.

'Maybe,' I said. 'But things are tough enough as it is without dragging a ball and chain around. Leave her behind, and we have one less pursuer to worry about.'

Anna started to cry.

'Oh, great! Turn on the waterworks again, why don't you,' I said. 'Like that's going to get us anywhere.'

'Okay!' said Vandersteen. 'That's enough! You can stop putting her down and you can stop your blubbering. We're going to walk for one more hour, and then we'll see where we are, and that's an end of it. Jesus fucking Christ Almighty!'

Anna looked up.

'And say one word about my language, and I'll bop you one!'

Anna closed her eyes.

When our hour was up, we were standing in the middle of a country lane, with a farm on either side. Sheets of rain were washing over us. Rain was good: it meant there wasn't a soul out and about. I was soaked to the skin and my feet were beginning to feel raw and sore.

'This is as far as we go,' said Vandersteen. 'What now?'

'I'm dead beat,' I said softly, in the hope that Anna wouldn't hear.

'I can keep going,' said Anna. 'No problem.'

I couldn't tell whether she meant it, or if she could sense I was at the end of my tether.

We walked on.

A few miles down the road, I was a wreck. My feet were blistered and throbbing like mad. There was a crease in one of the three socks on my right foot. I had already taken them off and put them back on again, but there was no getting rid of it.

'You're not taking that boot off again?' said Anna.

'Standing still won't help,' said Vandersteen.

As soon as we set off again, a knife-edge of pain slashed my heel.

'I'll manage,' I said.

We walked a little further. My hip started to ache, payback for trying to keep the weight off my crippled foot. I stopped again. Anna looked at me.

'Are you okay?' she said.

'Oh, shut up,' I said.

'I mean it,' she said.

I fought back the tears.

'If you're not able to go on, we should stop.'

'No, I'll manage. Really.'

The other two got into their stride once more.

The rain had finally stopped. I'd been biting back the pain since our last break, over an hour ago. My right foot had dissolved into a seething, stinging clump, and my left had gone to sleep. I flopped down on the sodden moss. My whole body felt like an old steamed pudding. Vandersteen had already scurried off to hunt down a squirrel or a bird. Where the hell did that woman get her energy? I picked my laces loose with trembling fingers and peeled the wet socks from my feet. The last sock on my right foot was sticky with blood and blister fluid. One of the blisters had burst.

'I've spent weeks in hospital, covered in blisters,' I said.

'And I still can't bear to look at them.'

'This is all part of it, eh?' said Anna.

'What?' I said grumpily. 'The pain? The misery? The blisters? The fact that you're worse off than me?'

'The fighting,' said Anna.

I wrung out my sock. The cold wind on my feet was bliss. Cautiously, I wiggled my toes. Heaven.

'Yes,' I sighed. 'It's all part of it. No friction, no progress.'

'I know that.'

'Yes,' I said.

'I'm not just a sad case.'

'No,' I said. 'You're not.'

'D'you want me to prick your blisters and tape up your foot?' Anna asked.

I nodded. She wrapped my foot in three layers of tape. We sat there in the dark and waited for Vandersteen.

She popped up out of nowhere, stealthy as a ninja, holding two dead squirrels by the tail. She plonked them down beside me, pulled handfuls of dry twigs and leaves from her pockets, and proceeded to make a fire, blowing gently on the leaves and twigs till they started to burn. She glanced around, stood up, snatched the squirrels from the moss, dropped them in my lap, and strode back over to the smoking fire. I started skinning.

The others were still asleep. I couldn't hear a motorway, I couldn't hear anything at all. My stomach was aching. I struggled up till I was sitting cross-legged and poked my foot out of the wet sleeping bag. Along the edges of the tape, my foot had begun to swell. I prodded it ginger-ly. New blisters had appeared beneath the tape, which was bulging like a tyre that's fit to burst. I looked up between the leaves at the sky above us. It would be a while before darkness fell. I shook Vandersteen gently till she was awake.

'My feet are all to buggery,' I said.

Vandersteen swore, and burrowed down deeper into her sleeping bag.

'I don't think I'll be able to walk very far tonight,' I said.

'It won't be dark for ages,' she mumbled. 'Get some sleep.'

'I can't sleep,' I said.

'Begging your pardon,' said Vandersteen. 'What I meant to say was: let *me* get some sleep.'

It was late in the afternoon by the time Anna and Vandersteen crawled out of their sleeping bags. The sun was shining and it was warm. The damp around us was slowly evaporating. I sat with my back against a tree trunk, and Vandersteen inspected my toes.

'What a mess,' she muttered.

She picked a corner of the tape loose and carefully unwound it.

'I've been thinking,' said Vandersteen. 'What if we were to actually get in touch with Mariska Kampschreur and her pack of newshounds?'

'What do you mean?' said Anna.

'What if we call her and tell her our story? Just like she said when she made her appeal.'

'Mariska Kampschreur is not above the law,' I said.

'Neither is Anna's brother,' said Vandersteen.

'My brother is beyond the law,' said Anna. 'That's something else entirely.'

'But that's exactly it: giving our story to Kampschreur is a way of exposing Anton.'

'My story.'

'Your story,' said Vandersteen.

'I don't want to tell my story.'

'You don't understand,' said Vandersteen. 'By bringing the truth out into the open, we'd be playing our winning card.'

'You just want to get your face on TV and your hands on that Kampschreur woman,' Anna scowled. 'I'm not selling my soul to the devil. All that talk about how you hate the law of the jungle, but you just can't wait to put me at the mercy of some bimbo off the telly. Well, you can sell her your own story. See where that gets you.'

I eyed up Vandersteen. I could see her making a lasting impression on the viewing public, all right. Anna began to cry. This club of ours was driving me up the wall.

'Why don't we sleep on it,' I said soothingly.

Vandersteen straightened her glasses and carried on fiddling with my foot. All my reasons for hating clubs so much began to rear their ugly heads. When we'd been in hospital and decided we belonged together, it had all seemed so logical, like a marriage.

'So why *did* you set fire to that newspaper yesterday?' asked Vandersteen. 'What did that article say?'

She let go of my toes, took off her glasses, and snapped them shut. The look she gave me was long and searching.

'What's brought all this on?' I said.

I felt a fluttering in my stomach. Vandersteen moved closer and crouched down until her face was inches from mine. She took hold of my chin.

'Ah-ha! Now I see. I knew from the start there was something about you, but I couldn't quite put my finger on it. For a while I thought you'd just been bullied, like any normal kid, but that's not it. Now I see. You were only a child when they locked you up.'

I struggled to free my chin. Vandersteen rose to her feet.

'Locked me up? Locked me up?' I said. 'What the hell are you talking about?'

'Is any of what you've told us true?'

I crossed my arms and held them tight against my chest.

'That's enough,' I said in a loud voice.

I could see birds taking flight in the distance.

'I know all I need to know,' said Vandersteen, and went back to taping up my foot.

I got lost that summer on the island. An omen of things to come, I sometimes think, looking back. It was also the first time it dawned on me that my mother thought I was a strange child. My parents wanted to go for a bike ride and I didn't want to go with them.

'Why don't you come along anyway?' said my father.

I sat there with my back against the shed and shrugged. I wanted to hang around the house, wander through the woods, and work on my animals at the workbench in the shed. My mother's favourite pastime was whiling away the hours at an outside table of some café. She'd nudge me and point out odd little things that caught her eye. But I couldn't do it anymore, play happy families. It wasn't till I was older that I realized how deeply that troubled my mother.

They left without saying a word. It was the first time they had left me at home alone. Perhaps they'd talked it through beforehand, as a milestone in my upbringing. Let's leave her behind and see how much she really likes it.

The first thing I did was eat crisps. When you're ten years old, your whole life revolves around sweets and crisps. I stood on a kitchen stool with the door of the crisps cupboard open and ate them straight from the bag. Cheese and onion. My fingers turned yellow. Then I downed a big tumbler of orange squash in two or three gulps. Then nothing much happened for a while. I sat there, thought about my parents, and waited for them to come back. Suddenly I started feeling very sorry for myself, sitting there alone on the settee, balancing the biggest tumbler in the cottage on my knee. I felt a bit queasy. That was when I jumped on my bike and began to pedal.

I couldn't find my parents. The cycling was wearing me out, but I kept my spirits up by singing to myself, and every so often someone would say hello. When I reached the village, I walked up and down the bustling high street. I felt like I was being watched. When you're a child, everyone has the right to stare at you, that's just the way it is, and when you grow up to be a woman, nothing much changes. I cycled into the woods. It was cool there, and my bike began to creak a little. My face was glowing from the sun and my bottom was sore from the saddle. I decided to get off and sit down for a while. I walked deeper into the woods and let my bike fall against a bush next to the path. The moss was soft. It was a lovely day.

I'd rest here for a bit and then cycle home. My parents would be back by the time I got there.

When I opened my eyes, it was dark. I had no idea where I was. I leaped up and began to run, then suddenly remembered my bike. I ran back, but I couldn't find it anywhere. The feeling that everything was small and neat and orderly had vanished completely. The cycle path was nowhere to be found. I stood still and sniffed my fingers. They smelt of soil, the blood on my knee, and a hint of the crisps I had munched down in secret. Thinking back, I can never quite get that moment into focus. It was almost animal. The urge to sniff my fingers was uncontrollable, as if that would make things better somehow. I got back to the cottage hours later—dirty, covered in scratches and cuts, and without my bike. I was so glad to be out of the woods. Walking up the path, I could see light shining from the window. I thought everyone would be happy to see me.

My mother was furious.

'Where have you been all this time?' she shouted.

I told her I had lost my way. She pulled me by the arm, dragged me over, and shoved me up the stairs. The next day, my father told me I had to go and play with the children from the neighbouring cottages. He said it would be more fun, and better for me than being on my own, or hanging around with them all day.

'So, these are your birds,' said the girl from the neighbours' cottage.

Her family had only just arrived, and my mother had

told me to go and make friends with their daughter.

'I thought you meant real birds.'

We were standing in the shed, looking at my island birds.

'They are real birds,' I said.

'I mean live birds,' said the girl next door.

'They were live... once,' I said.

She let out a squeal.

'What about this one?' she shouted.

She pointed at the pigeon I was working on. I explained it to her. How I made the form, how I cleaned the skin, the things you had to watch out for. Every little step was important, even with a fat pigeon like this one. All animals are equal that way. I showed her the glass eyes I used. Gently I stroked the feathers on the bird's little head.

'Aw,' said the girl next door. 'That's sweet.'

'It is, isn't it,' I said.

She looked at me and smiled. I knew something wasn't right, but as long as someone's smiling at you, there's not a lot you can say. She suddenly remembered she had promised to be home on time, and ran out of the shed. I thought no more of it and carried on with my pigeon. All told, I was glad she'd finally buggered off.

My parents announced that they were going to take a walk into the village. I was standing on a crate at the workbench and pretended not to hear them.

'Are you going to spend all day in this dingy shed again?' said my mother. 'With those filthy creatures?'

I nodded.

'I won't wander off,' I said. 'I promise.'

'Okay,' said my father. 'We won't be long. We'll be back in time for coffee, and we'll bring cake. Would you like that?'

My mother stroked my hair.

'Why don't you ask the girl next door if she wants to come out to play?' she said, turning her face away from the dead bird on the workbench. 'Other girls go horse riding, you know.'

'Leave her be,' said my father. 'She's finally found something she likes.'

'Honestly! Is this normal for a child of ten?'

My father took her by the hand. Things would all work out in the end. I carefully shaved the Styrofoam form with a gouge. This was going to be a lovely specimen, I could tell already. A nice, plump, lazy pigeon! The most comical bird ever! I was beaming with pride as I worked away, till something thumped against the back of my neck. Lumps of soil spattered across the bench. I heard giggling and spun around. I stepped off the crate and shook the soil from my jumper. The girl next door was standing in the doorway of the shed, flanked by two other kids. They let fly with more clods of earth. I ducked to avoid them.

'What did I tell you?' shouted the girl next door. 'Here she is—Frankenstein!'

'Frankenstein!' the other kids chimed in.

Children are like real people, only dumber. I told them to leave, but they wouldn't. They kept following me around, and when I sat down, they stood and stared at me. My parents came back in time for elevenses, and we all had cake. Everyone was cheerful and on their best behaviour, as if nothing had happened. The other kids—a pair of weasel-faced boys—turned out to be the girl next door's cousins. My parents had no idea there was anything wrong.

From a clump of trees at the edge of a field, we peeked out at the glare of the petrol station, watching the comings and goings.

'Not very busy,' said Vandersteen, polishing her glasses with a corner of her fleece. 'I don't know whether that's a good thing or not. We're looking for someone who needs a bite to eat or who's bursting for a pee. Someone in a hurry who'll forget to lock the car.'

I pulled the tobacco pouch from Vandersteen's jacket pocket and began to roll a cigarette. She had decided that we needed to get ourselves a car. I'd suggested asking a trucker for a lift, but that plan got voted down, two to one. Vandersteen had taken the lead, which was as it should be.

'Now!' she yelled, jumping across the ditch that bounded the field. I hobbled after her and just made the other side. Anna wasn't so lucky, and lolloped along behind us with one wet leg. A motorbike and sidecar was standing next to the petrol pump, engine throbbing and the nozzle of the pump wedged in the petrol tank. The tank had just reached full, and the pump shut itself off automatically. There was a little dog in the sidecar, no leash, no nothing. It was just sitting there, waiting, dozing off to the vibrations of the engine. The owner had stepped off the forecourt and lit himself a big fat cigar.

'Fuckfuckfuckfuck,' I muttered.

With every step, my right ankle was threatening to give up the ghost. Vandersteen had already reached our target, yanked the hose from the tank, straddled the saddle, and revved up the engine. Anna bowed her head and ducked into the sidecar. The little dog let out a short, sharp yelp. Still limping, I threw myself onto the bike, grabbed Vandersteen's backpack, and clung on for dear life. The biker bellowed and started charging toward us. Vandersteen slammed down her foot, and we shot across the forecourt and up the access ramp toward the motorway. I looked around at the bright lights of the petrol station and saw the biker stamp his feet and throw down his cigar in a fit of rage. Flames sprang up. People began to run and dive for cover. A massive explosion followed. The force of the blast propelled us forward. I buried my face in Vandersteen's backpack. When I looked back again, the petrol station was ablaze, flames shooting in every direction. We hit the motorway. Next to me, Anna was flailing about in the sidecar, trying to turn around for a look-see.

The little dog perched on Anna's lap and stuck its nose proudly into the wind, ears flapping, as we sped over the dyke. It gave a little bark. A church bell rang in a village down to our right, behind the dyke.

'If we keep going non-stop, we can reach the island in no time!' Vandersteen shouted over her shoulder.

I recalled the linen cupboard that contained my mother's clothes, the clothes I wore as a child, the white sheets and the blankets. Our attic beds, and how the roof used to creak when the wind raced across the island. Vandersteen started humming her Singing Nun song again. From the bike we could almost look down on the roofs of the villages we passed, and for every one, a steep little road swung down from the dyke. The sidecar bobbed at the dip ahead of every side road, and we almost seemed to dance as Vandersteen swerved just a little to compensate. As she sang, her voice grew louder, and Anna joined in, timidly at first. Before I knew it, I was singing along, too, in phonetic nonsense-French. Our voices rose till we were singing at the top of our lungs. Vandersteen's usual rasp was gone, her voice now high and reedy, Anna sang shy harmonies, and I warbled along as best I could. Then the bike hit a particularly deep dip ahead of the next side road, and the sidecar sprung loose. Anna screamed as she veered off and hurtled down toward the village below. The little dog still had its nose in the air, as if this was all part of the plan. I screamed in Vandersteen's ear.

'Fu-u-uck!' she yelled.

We looked down to see the sidecar rolling into the village. Vandersteen slammed on the brakes and gave a sharp tug on the handlebars. I clung on for all I was worth, but there wasn't much of her to hold onto. In what felt like a ten-point turn, she edged the bike forward and then back, like a wayward granny on her first mobility scooter. Facing in the right direction at last, we sped back along the dyke at full throttle and skidded around the hairpin bend down into the village.

'I can't see her!' I yelled.

We rode along between the houses, our engine sputtering away.

'You look left, I'll look right,' Vandersteen shouted.

Neat rows of lit-up houses shot past, and in no time we were out the other side of the village. Riding on past a pig farm, we spied the little dog shivering at the roadside. Vandersteen slammed on the brakes. Up ahead, in the shadow of a truck, a tall man was helping Anna out of the sidecar. She had smashed into the back of him.

Vandersteen switched off the engine. The little dog came padding along behind us. Anna stood there, looking dazed, but signalled to us that she was all right.

'What's the damage?' said Vandersteen to the trucker.

He peered under his truck.

'None that I can see,' he said.

The trucker towered above us. I reckoned he must be well over six feet, and in his late forties. From somewhere among his mop of blond curls, blood had started to trickle down his forehead.

'Your head—it's bleeding,' I said. 'Was it the collision?'

The trucker ran his fingers across his brow.

'Oh, that! Story of my life. Always banging my head on something.'

Vandersteen and I rolled the sidecar onto the verge at the side of the road.

'Pile of junk,' said the trucker. 'Death trap, if you ask me.'

He thought for a second. 'You're those three women on the run, aren't you? Your reputation precedes you. They're even flogging "Shhhh! I'm the Third Woman" T-shirts down at the local market. I got wind of you before you hit the headlines. You're the talk of the CB radio.

I'm not a great one for the news. They talk bollocks most of the time.'

'Are you going to call the police?' Anna asked.

The trucker started to laugh.

'You three have acquired hero status since François spread the word.'

'Ah,' said Vandersteen. 'Us and François go back a long way.'

We all shook his hand. He looked at Anna.

'According to the news, this one can't talk,' he said. 'The Third Woman.'

'That's me!' said Anna.

'And you're the one that bumped off her husband,' he said, turning to me.

'It's all a bit more complicated than it seems,' said Vandersteen.

'Isn't it always,' said the trucker. 'Like I said, the news is a bunch of bollocks.'

'I don't even know myself anymore what's true and what's not,' I said.

'What are you going to do now?' said the trucker.

'Start walking again,' I said.

'Unless we can get The Third Woman here back in the sidecar,' said Vandersteen.

'I'd keep off the roads if I was you,' he said. 'You're all over the TV and radio. When I looked into the sidecar and saw your burns, I knew right away who you were. Everyone knows, and not everyone's a trucker. Even the politicians are getting in on the act.'

He rubbed his forehead again, gave his fingertips a puzzled look, then rested his hands on his hips.

'I'll be off, then,' he said. 'Good luck.'

'Thanks,' I replied, as we shouldered our packs and put our best feet forward.

The trucker climbed into his cabin. I was hobbling along: every limping little baby step hurt. Behind us, we could hear the throb of the truck's engine. Slowly it pulled up alongside us and the trucker rolled his window down.

'Is there something wrong with your foot?'

'We're all a bit the worse for wear, right about now,' said Vandersteen.

'Tell you what,' said the trucker, 'I might be able help you on your way, just for a bit, like. I could use the company. Only I'm not having that filthy mutt in my cabin.'

We piled into the truck. I got in first, then Anna. Vandersteen ended up squeezed against the window on the passenger side. We left the trembling little dog behind.

'What a stink,' said the Tall Trucker. 'Even without the dog.'

He wound down his window again.

'By the way, did you have anything to do with that explosion about an hour ago? Over at the petrol station?'

'Explosion?' said Vandersteen. 'Nah… Not our style. I like your truck. Nice classic feel to it.'

The Tall Trucker patted the dashboard.

'This car used to be my dad's. Us drivers call them cars, not trucks. She's a monster, this one. Slurps petrol like there's no tomorrow, and the cap and those horns on top mean there's viaducts she won't fit under. But you can hook any old trailer up to her, so what more do you want?'

'Nice one,' said Vandersteen.

The Tall Trucker pointed at Vandersteen's door.

'Wind down your window, too, will you?'

He waved in some air. A crackling started coming from the dashboard, followed by the sound of distant voices.

'The sweet sound of 27 megahertz,' said Vandersteen. 'Are we hitting the headlines on the Citizens' Band, too?'

'Are you kidding? If news travels fast anywhere, it's on the truckers' hotline. If there's an incident anywhere in the country, everyone knows within five minutes. We're a tight-knit bunch. You wouldn't believe the gossip. Truckers are a bunch of old women, given half a chance.'

'What is that thing, exactly?' asked Anna.

'CB radio? It's a kind of walkie-talkie that connects you to other trucks within a certain radius. You can warn each other about tailbacks, checkpoints, accidents. We keep most of the gossip for our mobile phones these days.'

'Shame,' said Vandersteen.

'Shouldn't you three be laying low for a while? The way things are, you can't show yourselves on the street,' the Tall Trucker said. 'You know what? I was just on my way home. I live in a flat upstairs from Martha's. Ever heard of Martha's Bar?'

He filled us in. Martha's Bar was a great little place, centrally located, the perfect watering hole for weary drivers. We could take a shower at his place, wash our clothes, and get some shut-eye. He had a couple of spare mattresses we could bed down on. At the word 'mattresses,' every muscle and bone in my body began to cheer.

'I'll let you in on a trade secret,' said the Tall Trucker.

'The best truckers' cafes are found well off the motor-way.'

'Tell me something I don't know,' Vandersteen drawled, leaning her elbow in the open window.

From the car park at the back, I peered warily through Martha's window. A couple of men were slouched over their beers at the bar. The Tall Trucker gave a short whistle and waved us over. We followed him up a metal fire escape to the first floor. Inside his simple flat, he threw his keys on the table and ushered us into the living room with a flourish.

'Be it ever so humble… ' he said.

He opened a door.

'Toilet, shower, washing machine, dryer. Towels are in the white cupboard.'

Vandersteen flopped down on the couch. Anna wandered into the bathroom. I began pulling my clothes out of my backpack.

'Nice to see you making yourselves at home,' said the Tall Trucker.

'Do you drive the international routes?' asked Vandersteen.

'No, don't work enough hours, more's the pity. What do you do for a living?'

I looked up from my dirty laundry.

'Oh, all sorts,' said Vandersteen. 'This, that, little bit of the other.'

'You'll never get a straight answer from that one,' I said.

'Of course, I know all about you three by now,' said the Tall Trucker.

'Even though the news is a bunch of bollocks,' said Vandersteen.

'Got me there!' said the Tall Trucker cheerily. 'For example, I know you set fire to your houseboat and your husband. And you,' he turned to Vandersteen, 'escaped from a mental ward and called in that massive bomb scare at the station and then...'

'Okay, okay, okay,' said Vandersteen. 'You've made your point.'

Vandersteen and I locked eyes.

'Houseboat up in flames,' said Vandersteen. 'Well, well. An arsonist.'

'Escaped from a nuthouse?' I retorted. 'So much for your soap opera about Angelique and her ultimatum.'

'Oops,' said the Tall Trucker. 'Sorry. I thought you'd know all about one other by now.'

'Certain members of our little club have a habit of setting fire to things... including newspapers,' said Vandersteen.

'Don't worry, there was nothing in the paper about you,' I said. 'Don't go getting ideas above your station.'

I went back to sorting my washing. Anna came out of the bathroom. Vandersteen got off the couch and flashed the Tall Trucker a smile. Thanking him again for his hospitality, she strolled into the bathroom with her backpack.

'This is nice,' said the trucker. 'Having folk about the place.'

'Hmm,' I said. 'Depends on the folk...'

Washing my hair with the shampoo I'd found on the little shelf in the shower, suddenly I could smell Nelis. I picked up the bottle and looked at the label. I didn't recognize the brand, but when I closed my eyes, it was like he was standing there next to me. The washing machine was spinning away and I could hear voices coming from the other room, but for a few seconds I was home and it all came flooding back. The rocking of the boat, Nelis's voice, all the years I spent there. Footsteps across the floor, happy times. It seemed such a long way away. I stood there for a while, head bowed, hair white with foam, shower jet pummelling my backbone. A long, long way away.

The Tall Trucker suggested we go downstairs for a bite to eat. There would only be friends and people he knew in the bar, so it wouldn't be a problem. Martha could take any secret to the grave, of that he was sure.

'You know what I've been wondering,' said Anna, after the Tall Trucker had steered us toward a corner table behind the pinball machine, in the shade of a big potted plant.

'Well?' said Vandersteen, lighting a cigarette.

'Why didn't we just head straight across the border into Germany?'

It was quiet for a moment. I took a deep breath, ready to shoot my mouth off, but no words came.

'It suddenly occurred to me. I mean, we were right next to the border. Wouldn't it have been smarter to head east? Into Germany, and then on to Poland.'

Vandersteen gazed at her cigarette and blew smoke at the glowing tip. A big plate of bangers was served up with panache, like a five-star meal whipped out from under a serving lid.

'We just don't think straight,' said Anna. 'Instead of planning a getaway, here we are in a truckers' cafe, staring at a pile of sausages.'

'And so we stumble on our merry way,' said Vandersteen.

Creedence was coming from the speakers. It was always Creedence. 'Bad Moon Rising.' We tucked in, and for a while the conversation made way for chewing and smacking of lips. Anna slapped on the mustard.

'Then again, maybe it was smart, after all, not heading for the border,' Anna said eventually. 'Because everyone's assuming we do have a plan.'

Peering out from behind the leaves of the potted plant, I noticed every head in the place was turned our way. I ran my tongue across my teeth.

'Looks like we've outstayed our welcome,' I whispered, rubbing the bridge of my nose. 'Should we leave our stuff and run?'

One of the customers got to his feet. I tried to make eye contact with the Tall Trucker, who only now looked up at us. A bunch of men left their seats and started walking toward us. I jumped up and looked frantically for an escape route. The pain in my foot had vanished as if by magic. The closest door to us was the fire exit, which probably opened onto the side of the building. Unless it was locked, of course. This was exactly the kind of pub where they lock the fire exit to stop the clientele doing a runner. Anna and Vandersteen squeezed out from behind the table.

'Fire exit!' I shouted.

'Right behind you!' Anna yelled.

A trucker was standing between us and the door. Vandersteen shoved him out the way.

'What are you doing?' the Tall Trucker shouted.

The landlady was standing beside him, holding up three beers.

'We've all chipped in and bought you a round.'

Every trucker in the place began to clap. A standing ovation.

It was getting late, and there was no more coffee to be had. Martha nodded toward the coffee machine.

'Rinsed out for the night,' she said. 'I'd stick to beer if I were you.'

'I'll have a fresh orange juice,' Anna said.

We had all ended up at the bar. I'd arrived there by way of conversations with Henk, Johnny, Charlie, Jovink, and Verstegen. Even now, I'd be able to pick them out of a line-up without batting an eyelid. On my way, I'd slid all the newspapers I came across out of sight, as inconspicuously as possible.

'Nah, make that three beers,' said Vandersteen.

'So tell me, is she really... you know... normal?' Martha asked.

'What's up? Don't you serve beer to the mentally handicapped after ten?' said Vandersteen.

'Not in these parts,' Martha said.

'Of course I'm normal,' Anna huffed. 'Give it a rest, will you!'

'Just 'cause she's got a gammy leg doesn't mean she

can't drink beer,' said Vandersteen.

'I thought it was the other one who had the gammy leg.'

'I have trouble telling them apart sometimes,' said Vandersteen, and burped with her mouth closed.

'And she says she wants a fresh orange juice,' said Martha. 'Not beer.'

'Do you have fresh orange juice?'

'No.'

'Well, there you go, then.'

I sighed.

'Just pour the ladies a beer, will you,' said the Tall Trucker.

'If you say so,' said Martha. 'At least something's finally happened around here.'

'Yeah… like nothing ever happens around here,' said Charlie.

Martha put three beers down on the bar in front of us.

'Like what?' she said.

'Like when Frankie rammed his truck into them big flower pots out front,' said Jovink. He was sitting at the corner of the bar, staring at the TV like he was in his truck, staring at the road ahead.

'That was four years ago,' Martha said.

'Were they pretty flowers?' Anna asked.

'Meh,' said Martha. 'But it all costs money. That's when I started renting out rooms. If the gents get too drunk, I send them upstairs. They can have a bit of breakfast with my hubby and the kids in the morning. Some of 'em stay on. Like Tall Boy here.'

'We don't get sloshed often,' said Jovink. 'Got to hit the road again in the morning.'

'As I was saying,' said the landlady, 'nothing much happens around here.'

'What about the time that Frankie turned the fire hose on that creep who'd pissed out the upstairs window? Sprayed him clean out of the pub,' said a man who hadn't said a word so far.

'By rights, Frankie should be barred,' said Martha. 'But he's a good lad, so what can you do?'

The beer tasted good. Vandersteen and I took a final gulp and put our glasses down on the bar at the same time.

'Another?' asked the Tall Trucker.

'Are you going to pay their way all night?' said Martha.

'What's it to you?'

The landlady put one hand on the beer tap.

'What do *you* think?'

'Yeah, what do *you* think, Tall Boy?' said Vandersteen.

'I think the customer's always right.'

Martha filled three more glasses.

Vandersteen launched into a monologue about how she'd worked in this swanky lounge bar, serving German wine to a bunch of fat-necked execs.

'So this guy sez to me, "Yes, but what are we drinking, exactly?" And I sez, "How come?" 'Cause if it's a green bottle it's a Riesling, and that's all there is to it. So I sigh and point at the bottle and say, "What colour does that look like to you?" And he sez, "Yes, but what *Weingut* is it from?"'

Vandersteen was perched on her barstool like a seasoned comedienne, beer in one hand, cigarette in the other. The truckers were hanging on her every word.

'You know how it is,' said Vandersteen. 'Some folk ask you a question, but it's only so they can show off what they already know. They want an answer, all right, but they'll always come back at you. They always want the last word.'

The truckers nodded enthusiastically. Even Martha had slung her tea towel over her shoulder and was listening in.

'So I sez, "What *Weingut*?" And don't get me wrong, I'm a fan of German wine, I love German wine... Come to think of it, why the hell didn't we head for the German border when we had the chance?'

Dramatic pause.

'Not to worry,' said Vandersteen. 'Where was I? Oh yes, the idea that Germans only drink sweet plonk is hopelessly outdated. Germany produces plenty of fine, and above all, unpretentious wine. So he sez, "Yes, what *Weingut*?" And I sez, "Oh, how silly of me! Of course! *Weingut* is German for winery. Aren't you clever. This particular bottle's from *Weingut Yermasarightoldslappergunder*. Only this is the *Beerenauslese*." "Beg pardon?" sez yer man. "Is that a variety of *Spätburgunder*?" And I sez, "No, this is from Weingut Yer Ma's A Right Old Slapper. Gunder." "Well I never," sez yer man. He was just the type to say, "Well I never." Anyway, to cut a long story short, that was the end of my career at Helmut's Wine Bar.'

The whole pub cheered. The quiet bloke at the end of the bar slapped his thigh.

'But it was worth it,' she said. 'The look on that fella's face. He'd never heard the like.'

'Your glass needs attending to,' said the Tall Trucker. 'It's still half full.'

'Or half empty,' said Anna.

'Life in a nutshell,' said Jovink, eyes still glued to the telly.

We drank and drank. And drank some more.

The Tall Trucker kept putting his hand on my arm. I'd long since given up on the bandages. His touch should have been painful, but it wasn't. Anna and Vandersteen were bopping across the floor to the songs on the jukebox. Charlie was clapping along. It was all I could do not to fall off my barstool.

'Doesn't that hurt?' the Tall Trucker asked, looking down at his hand on my burned skin.

'No,' I said.

He kissed me. Martha turned on the disco lights. They were covered in cobwebs but they worked just fine. I began kissing the Tall Trucker back, and we took a break every now and then for a swig of beer. The landlady was in the mood for a dance, too. She stepped out from behind the bar and grabbed Charlie by the scruff of the neck.

In the Tall Trucker's hand, a regular beer glass looked like a kiddie tumbler.

'Tall men always find me more attractive,' I slurred, shouting above the music. 'Short men only see the double chin.'

Vandersteen popped up between us and leaned across the bar to pour herself and Anna another beer.

'Thasss jussss bollocks, Anna,' she jabbered. 'Isssss bollocks that women always hav't'ap-apologize for howdey-loook. Isss jusss nonsennsss, but peeeephull fink it really meanzzz sumfing. Peepuhl fink it'ssss sumfing you cun buy 'n' sell nnn meantime them bigwigs are jussss makin' money off my ins-hic-curities about myself… nnn all that… nnn you.'

'People only have themselves to blame,' said the Tall Trucker, putting his arm around me and pressing me against him. I let out a little yelp.

'Nnnnup,' said Vandersteen, 'dasss not true. If I tell you yer ugly the whole time… nnn yer not, yer not… nnn then I tell you the whole time that issss yer own fault and if there'sss nuff good-lookin' peeeephull who think issss yer own fault too… and I'm talkin' money here, I'm talkin' money… then issss ffffery diffficult to do anythin' about it. Nnn even good-lookin' people have to stay good-lookin'… nnn men… nnn that.'

She gazed at us, eyes zooming in and out, head bobbing like one of those little dogs in the rear window of a car. She picked up four full beer glasses from under the tap and planted two on the bar for us.

'See thisss woman here,' she said. 'I llluv 'er. I juss llluv 'er.'

She staggered back onto the dance floor.

The next afternoon I woke up in the Tall Trucker's bed with a crushing hangover. For a second, I didn't know where I was. Home, I thought, just for a second. Home, on the boat. It was the warmth under the quilt, the way the light filtered through the dark curtains. Everything was spinning. I'd slept like a baby, even the headache couldn't change that. I closed my eyes again. Spending the night with a man in exchange for a real bed—it seemed like a good deal to me. The trucker snuggled up to me. People just like sleeping together. Don't ask me to explain it.

'So,' he said, when he saw I was awake. 'Public enemy number one has regained consciousness.'

He told me everyone on the radio was most curious about Anna. That made sense, she was still a complete mystery. Vandersteen and I were battling it out for second place. I had done something really evil, while Vandersteen was the maddest member of our threesome. All kinds of bizarre rumours were circulating about her. She had spontaneously combusted. She had doused herself in petrol and set herself alight. She'd been torched by a gangster after defaulting on a loan. Everyone seemed to know her. Her wife and children turned out not to exist, or did they? As for me, I had blown up a houseboat full of innocent partygoers. But I wasn't mad. The Tall Trucker reckoned Vandersteen would end up last in our warped popularity contest. I pulled the duvet over my head and asked if he had any aspirin.

'Coffee, too,' he said, leaping out of bed. 'Just let me grab a shower first. There's aspirin in the bowl on the dining table.'

'Where are the other two?' I asked.

'They crashed on a mattress in the living room.'

I looked at the radio alarm clock. It was almost three. Only an hour or two before we were supposed to head off on foot again. I snuggled deeper into the downy folds of the duvet as the shower sprang to life.

It was warm and stuffy in the living room. The curtains were shut tight, and a sound like a rusty chainsaw was emanating from Vandersteen's sleeping bag. Anna was sitting bolt upright on her makeshift bed, staring at the TV. On the screen, a spokesman was speaking into an array of microphones. His face made way for images of police officers combing the vicinity of the petrol station.

'Slept like a baby,' I said, walking over to the table. 'How about you?'

'I was out for the count,' said Anna.

'I'm glad,' I said. 'Only now I have a splitting headache.'

'Me too,' said Anna.

'Want one?' I said, holding up the box of aspirin I'd fished from the bowl.

Anna shook her head.

'I'll be okay,' she said.

I filled a glass with water and swallowed two tablets. Then I went over to the mattress and sat down next to her.

'A proper mattress. What a luxury,' I said.

'Yes,' she agreed, eyes still fixed on the TV.

'What's on?' I said.

'We are,' said Anna. 'And they showed a photo. Of Leendert.'

'Your Leendert?' I said.

'Yes,' said Anna. 'But the sound was off. I didn't want to disturb Vandersteen.'

'But doesn't she sleep through everything?' I said.

'I couldn't reach the remote in time.'

'What did they say about him?'

'That's just it. I don't know. But there weren't any other

photos. I mean, none of me or Anton. I don't know what it means. They only showed it once.'

The Tall Trucker emerged from the bathroom, whistling. With a cheery 'good morning' he set about making coffee, and told us to make ourselves at home. At the first gurgle of the coffee machine, Vandersteen stretched and yawned. The Tall Trucker fried us up some eggs. It was all so warm and cosy. I thought of our mornings waking up in the woods and shuddered. Anna told Vandersteen what she had seen on TV.

'We can't stay here long. Especially not after last night's drinkathon. News travels fast, even with truckers for company,' Vandersteen whispered, and nodded toward the cooker.

'All things considered, it might not have been such a smart move to… '

She gave another nod in the Tall Trucker's direction.

'You know, start shifting your priorities.'

'Oh,' I said, miffed.

'Ah well,' said Vandersteen. 'Things happen. The main thing is… '

'And don't you start,' I said to Anna. 'The last thing I need is advice from a girl who picked up the man of her dreams in a fast-food place.'

'That was entirely different.'

'Oh yeah? And how was that entirely different?'

'That was love.'

Still whistling, the Tall Trucker came over with a plate of fried eggs.

'To be continued,' said Vandersteen.

We sat down at the table.

After breakfast, the Tall Trucker took his keys from the hook.

'Anyone fancy a little drive?' he said.

I looked up from the couch.

'Only one run to make today. Shouldn't take long.'

'In the truck?' I asked.

'Short trip, there and back,' he said. 'Just have to load her up and unload her in the next town along.'

I jumped to my feet.

'Don't tell me you're leaving again,' said Anna.

'What do you mean, "again"?' I said.

Anna crossed her arms. Vandersteen gave a little cough.

'Where's the harm in heading out for a bit?' I said.

'Well, put a cap on, for God's sake.'

'Want me to slap on a fake moustache while I'm at it?'

I asked the Tall Trucker if he had a cap. He laughed. Of course he had a cap. Quick as I could, I stuffed my things into my backpack.

'Truck drivers think they can do anything behind the wheel,' said the Tall Trucker, once we hit the motorway. 'Make coffee, read a book.'

I gazed out the window.

'We do a maximum of four fifteen-hour days and four nine-hour nights. The rest of the nights you're talking eleven hours minimum. Then we've got two ten-hour days while the rest are nine, with a max of four and a half hours in a row—behind the wheel, that is—split by a forty-five minute break.'

I couldn't help but yawn. The Tall Trucker nattered on

cheerfully as electricity pylons, fields, and cows rolled on past. The trucker always drove in his stocking feet to keep his cabin clean. He let me keep my boots on.

'Not boring you, am I?' he asked.

I shook my head.

'What day is it?' I asked.

'Wednesday,' he said.

'Wednesday already,' I said, as if it mattered.

The world was beginning to turn wintry. I started to feel the anxiety taking hold again.

'It's so easy to get used to things,' I said.

'Yes,' said the Tall Trucker. 'Hangovers excepted. Jesus wept!'

He wound down the window, stuck his head out, and adjusted his wing mirror. I wound down my window, too. Looking in the mirror I examined my cropped, tufty hair, the lines, scratches, and burns on my weather-beaten face. Who was this man sitting next to me? Nothing seemed to make any sense.

The Tall Trucker pulled up at a big warehouse and began loading the truck with pallets stacked with boxes. I stayed in the cabin with his cap pulled down to my eyebrows and fiddled with the radio. I wanted to hear what they were saying about us, about me. The news channel was banging on about South America, and all I could find on the other channels was music. Disappointed, I kept turning the dial. The clock told me it was another fifteen minutes till the news on the hour. I flipped back to the news channel. Looking out through the windscreen I saw more big company warehouses, and in the wing mirror I caught the occasional glimpse of people toddling past. I wondered what Anna and Vandersteen were doing around about now, and puzzled over what Anna had seen on the morning news. They could just as easily have mentioned Nelis and the boat, too. My partners in crime were bound to hear the whole story at some point. Perhaps it would be better coming from me than from some newsreader. I sat there and pondered. The idea of Anna and Vandersteen knowing what I had done filled me with shame. Not that I could help it. It was the way of the gallant south: act like nothing's happened as long as no one else knows about it. The mere thought that they might hear my darkest secrets read out on the news made my heart skip a beat, and I was ambushed by the fear that they would up and leave without me.

The news began at last and I turned up the volume. We were continuing to divide public opinion. One camp thought we were a disgrace to humanity, the other reckoned we were taking a stand. The petrol-station blaze was the talk of the day, but there was no mention of the man who owned the motorbike and sidecar we'd stolen, or his wayward cigar. Someone said he was intrigued by our decision to target the oil companies after we'd exposed a drugs operation. Someone else was fuming that we were still on the loose after all the public money that had been pumped into tracking us down. A politician said the commotion was simply a smokescreen to distract the electorate from the real issues affecting the nation.

I made a vow to tell Anna and Vandersteen everything when I got back, before we continued our journey. It was time to talk, or things would all go wrong. It doesn't take much to make things right. It's not about a plane looping 'I love you' across the sky. It's not about hiring a string quartet and getting down on one knee, not even about your parents giving you life, taking care of you, and paying your way. It's not in the grand gestures that are all about making a point, gestures that say, 'Look at everything I'm doing for you.'

It's in the moment when someone holds you and whispers softly, so softly you can hardly hear, 'I've missed you so very much.'

All I wanted was for the three of us to stay together.

I was standing at my father's side, watching the wild chickens at the edge of the woods. I had never seen them fly, though no one clipped their wings. At home, Hetty had pride of place on my bedside table.

'Do you like playing with the girl next door?' he asked.

I'm sure he must have called her by name, but I can't remember what it was. I can't even remember what it sounded like.

I nodded. My father looked relieved, and that made me feel relieved, too. In the end, it's all about how you make other people feel. At least, it is if you spend too long thinking about it.

My playmates came back the next day, all three of them. While my parents welcomed them with open arms, I tried to hide away upstairs. It was no good. My mother fetched me down from the attic.

'You have to make more of an effort,' she said. 'They're waiting for you in the garden, knocking a ball about.'

My mother came outside with a tray of goodies. After

tea and biscuits, my parents started to get ready for a walk on the beach. I said I wanted to go with them. I really, really wanted to go with them.

My parents laughed, and the other children said they'd much rather play in the shed. So my parents went off without me.

I walked slowly over to the shed, my tormentors following on behind me. It felt like a procession. I wanted to tell them to sit down in the corner and I would give them something to do, something fun. I wanted them to listen to me. I didn't say a word, but picked up a gouge from the workbench and carried on stoically where I'd left off.

'Ugh. It's like a horror film, only it's real,' said the girl next door.

She pushed me aside and grabbed the pigeon from my hands. The bird ripped at the seams. That was when I went for her.

When they came back from their walk, my parents found me curled up in a corner of the shed, cradling the remains of the pigeon in my jumper.

'I didn't do anything,' I said.

'Come here,' said my mother. 'Let's get this cleaned up.'

'I didn't do anything. Honest, I didn't.'

My mother took me into the bathroom. My father threw the pigeon in the bin. The road to hell is paved with vicious people, people who look you in the eye and smile and take you by the arm. Later, the woman next door came over to tell my parents that her daughter had a cut on her face, a cut that ran from her eye to her chin. She was scarred for life. I had attacked her with the gouge. I sat upstairs on my bed, listening in. The neighbours had gone to the police, even though they were well aware that I was not a normal child. That was my last day on the island. We took the ferry the same evening. Not long after, they put me in a home for a while, a place where I could learn to control my feelings.

It was still light when we got back to the Tall Trucker's flat. He decided to take a nap. I joined Anna and Vandersteen at the dining table. The TV was off, the radio, too.

'Right,' said Vandersteen. 'We need to work out where we go from here. I've been giving it some thought, and I've half a mind to get the press involved. Now that we're flavour of the month, it gives us the chance to explain to everyone in no uncertain terms exactly who mutilated that poor Third Woman they feel so sorry for. The other half thinks we'd be better off keeping our heads down and making a beeline for the island. No one has a clue where we're going. Then again, it might be smart to play the only trump card we have.'

'Anna,' I said.

I could tell from their expressions that they hadn't heard any new revelations on the radio. Vandersteen fiddled with the map in front of her on the table, looking at it from all angles. I thought about the vow I'd made to myself back in the truck, but now I wasn't so sure about the need to tell all.

We agreed to set off when darkness fell. At a stiff pace, there was every chance we could make the coast in two nights. With a little help from the trucker's old school atlas, we mapped out a route for ourselves. We were all nervous. I put on my coat and sat down on the couch to wait. Anna came and sat next to me. Then Vandersteen squeezed in beside us. She sat bolt upright with her backpack already on.

The room grew steadily darker.

'I don't want to die,' said Anna.

'We're not going to die,' said Vandersteen. 'Everything will be all right. You just need to be brave a little while longer. Why don't we have a bit of a chat? Isn't there something you always wanted to know?'

'Before we die, you mean?' I said.

'Oh, give over!' said Vandersteen.

'Did you really live in a toyshop?' said Anna, after a short pause.

Now it was Vandersteen's turn to think.

'Of course I've never lived in a toyshop,' she said, her voice suddenly much softer. 'Of course not.'

'So you made it all up?' said Anna.

'Oh, I've been telling that story for years. For centuries. As a kid, I never lived anywhere for more than a few months. That was bad enough. One day, when I was still a kid, it dawned on me that a toyshop might seem like the best place ever to live, but that if you actually lived in one, it probably wouldn't be all that much fun. That if you could just take anything you wanted, there would be nothing more to wish for. From that moment on, I began to tell the new children I met the story about the toyshop, and how it was no fun at all. Pretty philosophical for a kid, when you think about it. Went down a treat.'

It was quiet for a moment.

'I know you both understand,' said Vandersteen.

'I had a perfectly happy childhood,' I said.

'And one day I fell in love,' Vandersteen went on. 'With the most beautiful woman in the world. Prick up your ears, Anna and Anna, because I hate shitty stories like this. But it needs to be told, just this once. I fell in love with her and she fell in love with me. And it went the way these things always go. We moved in together, we were happy, we had children. I was so happy, I was fit to burst. And yes, I knew it couldn't last. I mean, when I'm alone, I even start to get on my own nerves. It's hard for everyone, and as for me, well… I grew up in a toyshop. I knew for certain she was going to leave me. I just knew. We were standing outside the house, next to the car. It was a couple of weeks after the bomb scare. There we were, standing next to my old, clapped-out Opel Kadett Coupé, and I'm loading my bags into the car, and she says it again, that she loves me but she can't be with someone who lies all the time. It's not right, she says, it's just not right, is it? I put the last of my bags in the boot and she wants to kiss me, but I pull back. Before her lips can touch mine, I stick my cigarette in my mouth and almost burn her cheek. She jumps, gives me a long look, then turns away and walks up the path. I take a couple of puffs on my cigarette without lifting a finger to touch it. And I think, you don't know me at all. Not at all. I take the jerrycan from the boot, screw off the top, open my lips, and let the cigarette fall. And there you have it… the shitty story of what happened to me. I saw her one more time in the hospital, late in the evening. She wanted to see how I was doing, she said. She could only stay a minute or two, hoped I'd be sleeping. I told her I was doing fine. I never saw her again. So that's that. Now you know. We all have something to hide. There's no harm in hiding. That's just the way it is sometimes.'

Vandersteen gave a flat laugh.

'I don't want to go on by myself,' I said.

Anna spread her arms and put them around our shoulders. I let myself slump against her. The living-room clock ticked on. I looked up at the hands. Three more hours of waiting.

Slowly, I drifted off to sleep.

'Anna,' Vandersteen whispered. 'Anna.'

It was dark. I mumbled something.

'They're here. We have to go.'

'Nah, not yet,' I mumbled. 'Another ten minutes.'

Vandersteen shook me to my senses.

'They're downstairs. The police are downstairs. Now.'

I was wide awake. Vandersteen slid the curtain a fraction to one side.

The Tall Trucker wandered sleepily into the living room.

'We have to go,' I said.

'They're downstairs at the pub, and one of them's parked at the bottom of the fire escape,' said Vandersteen. 'Our best bet is to climb over the balcony, sneak down, and head for the woods.'

We peeked through the crack in the curtains. I slung my backpack over my shoulder. Everything felt dry and

I felt rested. I circled my right foot. It still felt tight, but somehow I'd manage.

'Yes, the woods. That's our best option,' I said.

'Have you got the map?'

I patted the side of my backpack and nodded.

'I think they have dogs with them,' said Vandersteen.

Another police car pulled up and parked just out of view.

'It's not looking good,' said Vandersteen. 'They'll be up here before you know it.'

'Hey,' said the Tall Trucker.

The three of us hissed in unison.

'What if I get my truck?'

'Yes… and… ?' said Vandersteen testily.

'You can climb off the balcony onto the roof.'

He stood up and began to pull on his shoes. We looked at each other.

'Game?' asked Vandersteen.

'Game!' said Anna and I, at the same time.

The Tall Trucker stuck his head in among the three of us and planted a kiss on my cheek.

'I'll be right back.'

He took the keys from their hook, spun them around his finger like a revolver, and strode out of the room. Vandersteen disappeared behind the curtains. We heard her ease open the door.

'They're standing under next door's window,' she whispered.

I heard voices, but couldn't quite make out what they were saying.

Suddenly the curtains were bathed in light and I heard

the rumble of an engine. The light swung away and the truck came squeaking to a halt right alongside the balcony.

'Are you out of your mind?' someone under the window shouted. 'You nearly flattened us!'

The Tall Trucker apologized, muttered something about forgetting his wallet, and walked into the building. Vandersteen put one foot on the edge of the balcony and leaped onto the roof of the truck without a sound. No thump, no smack, nothing. I perched on the railing, turned carefully on my backside, and lowered my feet onto the truck. Vandersteen gave me a hand. Out of the corner of my eye, I caught sight of two policemen. One was gazing off into the distance, the other was examining his fingernails. I shuffled cautiously away from the edge of the roof. Then I turned toward Anna and stretched out my hand.

'Come on,' I said.

The Tall Trucker came back out of the building and greeted the two policemen. The curtains at the balcony doors lit up from inside, and the room filled with shadows. Anna hesitated.

'Lean your backside on the railing first,' I whispered.

Her backpack was getting in her way. I grabbed her hand, and at that moment the curtains were yanked aside. Anna launched herself and landed on the truck with a thud. The Tall Trucker started the engine and the policemen on the ground looked up. The doors flew open and a pack of coppers spilled out onto the balcony. The truck lurched into reverse, and we slid forward over the roof. One of the coppers tried to leap from the balcony but chickened out at the last minute. The truck sped off and gunshots rang out. I clawed my way to the edge of the roof and held on for all I was worth. We hit the motorway. I looked around and saw flashing blue lights coming closer. Anna and Vandersteen were at the other end of the roof, holding each other tight.

The wind howled in my ears. I crawled over to them. Vandersteen was deathly pale and lay like a doll in Anna's arms. Anna looked at me. Her face was covered in blood.

'They got her,' said Anna.

As the truck thundered on, we lay on the roof with our arms around Vandersteen. Under a viaduct the truck's engine ground to a halt with a dark thrumming bass, slow and deep. It rumbled in my chest as if it was part of my body, as if it was coming from inside me.

Now there were blue lights flashing up ahead, as well. 'Climb onto the viaduct!' the Tall Trucker yelled.

Police cars pulled up around the truck on all sides.

'Now!' he screamed.

We let Vandersteen go. We left her lying there. No goodbyes. Hanging onto a steel grid with traffic signs mounted on it, I heaved myself up. Anna hauled herself up next to me. I saw the Tall Trucker being bundled into a police car below us as coppers began to scale the side of the truck. A loud, tinny voice told us to stop and surrender or they would shoot. As soon as my feet landed on the viaduct I was all set to run when I heard someone call my name. A trucker flung open his cabin door. As we jumped in, I thought of Vandersteen lying there on the roof of the Tall Trucker's truck. I knew without a doubt that she was dead, though there are still times when I wonder. But then, there are times when I wonder if any of it happened for real. Vandersteen would have wanted us to go on. There are times when I wonder about that, too.

Further down the road, the driver let us out of his truck. We fled into the woods like a pair of stray dogs.

We forgot to eat. All we did was walk. I still had that Singing Nun song rattling around in my head. I even caught myself humming it a few times. Anna never joined in, the way she had when there were still three of us. It was hard to believe we had ever dared sing it at the top of our lungs. Anna didn't say a word the whole day after we had left Vandersteen lying on top of the truck. Somebody once told me it's best to travel in threes, but two is still better than being alone. I think I would have given up long ago if there hadn't been someone who needed me as much as Anna did. Perhaps that meant I needed her even more.

It felt as if we weren't getting any further north, as if we were walking in a dream. Between the trees I saw the light of an occasional lamppost in the distance, or a car turning onto a road. Every heartbeat echoed through the woods for all to hear. At first light we squeezed into a narrow gap along the side of an embankment and slept till the sky grew dark again.

'I could really do with a coffee.' They were the first words Anna spoke since we had left Vandersteen for dead. We had almost reached the coast.

'Me too,' I said, 'but we're so close now.'

'Leendert, now there was a man who liked his coffee,'

said Anna. 'He always had coffee on the go. Sometimes he'd already rinsed the pot when I came over late in the evening. But even then, there was usually a fresh brew to be had. "Home isn't home without a fresh pot of coffee," he always used to say.'

'Sounds familiar,' I said.

'When he made a fresh pot, he'd write down the time and leave the note next to the coffee machine.'

'He left a note with the time on it next to the machine?'

'Yes,' said Anna.

I bit my tongue.

'He was married, you know,' Anna said. 'I was too ashamed to tell you. Now it doesn't matter anymore. Now Vandersteen is gone.'

'What?' I said.

'I was so ashamed. I regret it, really I do. But he had an awful marriage.'

'What?' I said again.

'Sorry, Anna,' said Anna. 'That's a stupid thing to say. It doesn't matter how good or bad his marriage was.'

She wanted to touch me. I pulled back.

'No,' I said. 'Tell me again, about the coffee.'

Anna gave me a puzzled look.

'The coffee. Tell me about the coffee.'

'I don't understand,' she said.

'What did you say about the coffee?' I shouted. 'Did he live on a boat?'

'Did I tell you that already?' said Anna. 'I must have told you that already.'

'A houseboat,' I said. 'In the old docks. Next to the pig abattoir.'

'Yes!' Anna exclaimed. 'Leendert.'

He didn't even make much of an effort with his alias. Her Leendert and my Nelis were one and the same. She began to cry.

'Don't go turning on the waterworks!' I shouted.

'What do you mean?'

'He's dead. Your Leendert. He didn't know anything about what happened to you. Not a thing. So there you go. He's dead.'

I told her all about the boat. I told her everything. I even laid it on a bit thick. How happy I had been. How nice everything was, how good it felt to be on the boat. I could see the recognition in her face. She had felt good. She had been happy, too.

'And it never dawned on you for a second that it might have been me? With the stuffed birds? Who in God's name has a flock of stuffed birds at home? No one! Only me! Only me!'

'He never showed me your room!'

I didn't have an awful marriage. I didn't have an awful marriage. I had a fantastic marriage.

'I picked up the gas canister,' I said. 'I lit it. I can still see the expression on his face. Surprise. He knew I would never do something like that, and I did it anyway. Just like you. You would never have done what you did, either. You're a sly one, all right. I saw it all go up in flames, I fell into the water and I came out alive. As for you, you've only got yourself to blame.'

And I had her to blame. For everything.

'So what does that say about you?' Anna yelled. 'That he chose someone like me? What does that say?'

175

'Maybe you don't even have a brother,' I said. 'Maybe you're as big a liar as the rest of us. Vandersteen, Nelis, the whole bloody lot of us.'

'And the cock crowed three times,' said Anna.

I told her Nelis had a thing for chunky women, and that I'm chunky, too, but I was willing to bet she'd been even chunkier, before the fire. For a moment I felt a thrill flare up inside me again, the same thrill I'd felt when I saw them in bed together. Only for a moment.

I ran into the shadow of the woods. Anna called after me, but I kept right on running. I didn't look back. I fell and fell again, flat on my face among the wet leaves. The smell of soil and mould. Reaching out for tree trunks as I ran, hard roots beneath my feet, I stumbled on and reached the far edge of the woods. I was alone. A sandy plain stretched out in front of me. The white disc of the moon came and went behind the clouds. The wind was strong and sand spun through the air. Here in the night, the sand looked like it might go on forever. I wondered what the time was. Once in a while I thought I saw Anna, but there was no one, only low bushes and the odd tree. The wind grew stronger still, and I shielded my face with my hands. I thought I could make out where the plain ended and, with nothing else to give me my bearings, I kept on walking. My calves burned from ploughing through the shifting sand.

And then, out of nowhere, it seized me by the throat.

I felt sorry. I felt so very sorry.

Intense remorse spread like heartburn through my veins. I was sorry for everything. For everyone who had died, for everyone I'd left behind. Sweat covered me, my clothes clung to me, my mouth was parched. My stomach knotted, panic snatched at my breath. All the water I had inside me was pouring out. I had the sudden sensation of people closing in, breathing down my neck. Perhaps they had caught up with Anna already. I needed someone to forgive me. I walked on and words began to pound inside my head. 'Forgive me, please forgive me. I've done everything wrong. I don't want to be alone. I try and I try to face it on my own, I want to face it all but I can't, I can't. I've destroyed everything. I do everything wrong, I only think of myself. Forgive me, please. I need forgiveness. I will never think of myself again, I will always put others first, forgive me. I am a killer, an evil woman, no good to anyone. Forgive me, please, please forgive me. But don't leave me here on my own. Please don't leave me here alone.'

I fell to the ground.

Grains of sand were everywhere, swept up from the dusty plain. The clouds parted and the moon shone down. I got to my feet and turned around. I had to go back. When I reached the edge of the woods, I could no longer tell if I was really there. I looked for Anna. I looked for Anna and I could not find her. I slumped against a tree and my knees buckled. I curled up and pressed my weary body against the trunk.

'Annie?' A voice above me. 'Annie?'

I opened my eyes.

'All this time you've been lying here snoozing, thirty feet away?'

Vandersteen grabbed me by the arm and gave me a hug.

'Here you are,' she said. 'I was really worried about you.'

'I'm so thirsty,' I said.

Vandersteen pulled a bottle from her trouser pocket.

'Ditch water. So don't say I didn't warn you when you get the shits later.'

I gulped it down in a oner.

'Tonight you can have a bird,' said Vandersteen. 'You can have a whole bird to yourself.'

'I love birds,' I said. 'And it's cold without you.'

'Less of your whining,' said Vandersteen.

'Where's Anna?' I asked.

Vandersteen pointed between the trees.

'Over there,' she said. I saw a mound of sleeping bag, rising and falling in time with her breath.

'It changes everything.'

'It shouldn't change everything,' said Vandersteen.

A story can change while you're standing there, watching it unfold. A big fat pigeon landed beside us. It grunted. It should have cooed, but it grunted.

'You can go on making the same choices,' said Vandersteen.

'Is she still asleep?'

'I don't know.'

'Friends don't betray one another.'

'The important thing is what your intentions are.'

'Yes,' I said. 'We left you lying there on the roof of that truck.'

Vandersteen took a puff of her cigarette.

'Sorry,' I said. 'I'm sorry.'

'That's all right,' said Vandersteen.

I swallowed. It wasn't easy.

'Yes,' said Vandersteen. 'Spend all your time in your head, and who's going to take care of the rest of you? You're more than just a head. You know that, don't you? If you don't know that by now, we needn't have made this journey at all.'

'How come you know so much?' I said.

'Good advice is for giving away,' said Vandersteen. 'And Lord knows I've been given a shitload in my time. Enough to drive you bonkers. But it's yours now. It's all yours.'

It was all mine. The pigeon gave another grunt, and in a single motion Vandersteen reached down and grabbed it by the neck.

'Breakfast,' said Vandersteen, rising to her feet. 'And forgiveness. That, too.'

I sat up. A short distance away was a sleeping bag with Anna tucked up inside. I walked over to her. The twigs beneath my feet cracked, so did my knees. The folds of the sleeping bag hid her face. Peacefully the mound rose and fell, rose and fell. Way off to the left somewhere I thought I could hear a road, and in the distance I saw a cyclist pedalling down a bike track. Anna rolled over and opened her eyes.

'Hi,' she said.

'I'm here,' I said. 'It's time we moved on.'

'Yes,' she said. 'I had the strangest dream.'

'Oh,' I said.

'About Vandersteen.'

I sat down beside her.

'I'm hungry,' I said.

Anna nodded.

'Are things ever going to be all right?' she said.

'They already are,' I answered.

I smelled the sea before I saw it. We climbed up a low dyke and gazed out across the mudflats. We'd be able to reach the island in five hours. I didn't know how long it would take for the tide to come in, but I felt sure we would make it.

'We have to keep our eyes on the lighthouse and walk at a steady pace,' I said. 'Otherwise we'll have to swim for it.'

I chuckled. Anna put her arm round me. I rubbed my eyes and pressed my face to her shoulder.

'The first thing I'll do when we get there is brew us up some coffee,' I said into the fabric of her sleeve.

'No, first we'll change into clean clothes,' said Anna. 'So we can drink a fresh cup of coffee like decent folk.'

'Yes, like decent folk,' I said.

I grabbed hold of her and pressed her tightly against me. It was the last time I would feel her warm, fat body against mine. We heaved our backpacks into position and walked down to the beach.

'Not far now,' I said. 'It looks like the lighthouse isn't getting any closer, but that's just a trick of the light.'

Over my shoulder, I could no longer see the spot where we had come down from the dyke. I kept a tight hold of Anna's hand.

'In a little while, I'll light the stove in the cottage. There's bound to be a bag of rice and a tin of beans somewhere. Yes. Rice and beans. That's what we'll have. It's just the day for rice and beans. I'll light the stove and the oven, then I'll empty the tin into the pan. No, wait, first coffee.'

I could already see my fingers running along the little jars in the spice rack: tarragon, oregano, paprika, white pepper. The jars would be a little sticky, the herbs more grey than green.

'I'll make us rice and beans, and you can fetch water for the boiler. My father used to say, "Always fill the boiler while you're cooking, otherwise half the heat will vanish into thin air." You can be first in the bath.'

She didn't answer.

'Okay, Anna?'

Anna nodded. We had to hurry. The key to the cottage was hidden at the back of the shed, under the false bottom of the heavy oak chest, where my parents kept their tools. I can still remember my mother gluing in the false bottom. My parents weren't the kind of people to forget their keys, but they were the kind to fit a false bottom in a toolbox, just in case. My boots were heavy with water and my socks had soaked up as much as they could hold.

The tide was coming in. We waded up to our waists in water and barely spoke another word. We had taken off our boots and eventually we shook free of our backpacks—dead weight that could only slow us down.

It was already too late. We'd have to swim for it. I tied the sleeve of my jacket around my ankle, gave the other sleeve to Anna and told her not to let go, no matter what. As the black water rose higher, I kept my eyes fixed on the lighthouse.

'Not far now,' I yelled.

As long as I could feel her pulling on my ankle, we'd be fine.

'Can you hang in there? Anna?'

'I don't know,' she shouted.

'In a little while we'll be walking up the path to the cottage, and you can be first in the bath. And we'll eat rice and beans and drink coffee. And we won't have to think about everyone who's died. Not anymore. We'll be all right. The two of us, together, we'll be all right.'

She didn't reply. We were both out of breath.

'The bed will be nice and warm, and you can have the big bed. Some nights you can hear an owl in the woods. I'll leave the skylight open for you, and in the morning I'll make breakfast, and no one will know where to find us, no one will know where we are. No one, just you and me, and we won't talk about any of it anymore, okay? We'll mean what we say and say what we mean. There will only be now. Only now. Only now.'

A wave washed over me. I began to cough.

'Anna.' Her voice behind me. 'Anna.'

We held onto each other. Wave after wave washed over us. We went under.

'Don't let go of me,' said Anna, when we surfaced again.

'Never,' I said.

'I have to forgive Anton,' she said. 'Forgive him before we die.'

'We're not going to die,' I said.

'Please don't let go of me,' she said.

We went under again. Deeper this time. Anna thrashed and floundered and I became tangled in the jacket. I needed air. I needed air. I shook off the sleeve, pushed her away, and struggled up toward the light, clawing at the water above me. I broke the surface, took a great gulp of air, and swam on. Alone.

I sank to my knees in front of the cottage. After all these years, there was hardly anything left of the place. I staggered around the remains. The shed had been reduced to its foundations, and someone whose name I would never know had carried off the old oak chest. The woods had crept steadily closer. I lay on my back and looked up through the twigs and branches at the clouds that blew over. I had seen it all in my mind's eye: how I would return here, how everything would be as it had always been. It had never occurred to me that it might all have rotted away to nothing. I never imagined such a thing could happen. No one had thought to tell me. I had never thought to ask.

That was when I heard the cackling. I tilted my head to the right and looked toward the woods. There was nothing to see, but the cackling grew louder. I looked up at the sky again and then I saw them, above me in the branches. High above, perhaps fifteen feet off the ground. The sun was rising, the cackling grew louder still, and when the first ray of light touched the edge of the woods, they launched their heavy bodies. The branches swayed to and fro behind them. They flew over me—there must have been ten at least. I closed my eyes without knowing where they landed.

Then the world went black.

Beep… Beep… A machine beside me. I opened my eyes and tried to sit up.

'You're alone,' said the nurse. 'You're a lucky lady. You're doing fine.'

'Is everyone dead?' I asked.

'No, we're alive and well,' said the nurse. 'All you have to do is press that button there, Mrs Van Veen. Now, try to get some sleep. It's the middle of the night, you know.'

'Is there someone outside the door?' I said.

'Yes,' she said. 'There's someone outside the door. Just as well, too. There's quite a commotion out there. You're on the top floor. I'll open the curtains for you in a little while. In a few hours' time you'll have some visitors, people who want a word with you about what's next. When we can move you, that sort of thing. Can I get you anything else? Some magazines? A newspaper? On second thought, perhaps a newspaper's not such a good idea. Makes no difference to me, mind. I treat everyone the same. Just so you know, Mrs Van Veen. I like to keep up with the news.'

I shook my head and the room started to spin.

'Do you have a notepad?' I asked.

She smiled and fished a thick little pad from her trouser pocket, along with a pen.

'Here,' she said. 'I've only torn out a page or two. It's all yours.'

I didn't ask what was going to happen next. Instead, I

took hold of the pad and began to count the pages. There were two-hundred and forty-eight. I counted them often, so I know for sure. Twelve lines a page.

'You're alone. You're a lucky lady. You're doing fine.'

I've never been good with numbers. All I know is that the dyslexic hearts club still exists, except now I'm the only member. The only one here. I don't know how many days we spent on the run, or how many days we spent together in the confines of that hospital room. But I'm so glad I was part of it all, so glad I didn't miss a single one. Anna and Vandersteen—sometimes it seems like they never really existed. Because the sun comes up and the day begins. And day becomes night and night becomes day. And I go on living, in a straight line toward the end, just like everyone else. That's what binds us, what makes us human. We are alone and all we have to do is find a way to forgive ourselves for everything. I know that, don't I? All the love I have inside me is pouring out. I feel it all, feel everything, I feel for everyone who knows what it is to love. And that will make everything all right. Time is a road shooting past under your wheels. Vandersteen is in the driver's seat, and I'm sitting next to her, and the asphalt stretches on ahead of us and shoots out from beneath our wheels. The sun is shining and this road we're on seems to thunder through the trees right along with us. Beside me I can feel Anna's warm body. She's sleeping with her cheek pressed up against the window and it's just the three of us, and I'm so happy I'm fit to burst. The engine hums and the traffic races past. Sometimes Anna snores a little, when the truck takes a bend, when we peel off at an exit to join another motorway. Vandersteen starts to sing, humming softly at first, in a reedy, high-pitched voice. It's the song of the Singing Nun—*Dominique-nique-nique*—and I sing along. I sing and the asphalt is wet with rain, wet with the rain of days gone by, those rivers of water that fell on us, and we are light and we are happy and no one hurts. The sun is shining, we squint into the brightness of the shimmering asphalt and I feel Anna beside me and I listen to Vandersteen, her voice suddenly high, soaring free of her rasp and her cough. We are driving with nowhere to go.

The sun is shining and the birds are singing at the top of their lungs and we are happy. And it's a beautiful day, my friends.

It's a beautiful day.

This novel would never have seen the light of day without the unfailing help of Lotte Lentes, Dennis Gaens, and Ad van den Kieboom. Thanks to Stijn Raven, Marcel Bogerman, and the men of Lewiszong Transport for their advice on matters such as three suspected criminals sharing a hospital room and the wondrous world of the truck driver. Additional thanks go to Nina Dörner, whose apartment in Berlin is a second home to me now, and the lovely, lovely people from Café In de Blaauwe Hand. Almost every page of this book was written at your tables.

And without Dorus van de Burgt I would have gone crazy three times over while writing this book. Just so you know.

For more information, visit us at www.worldeditions.org.